IMITATION

HEATHER HILDENBRAND

IMITATION

alloyentertainment

Produced by Alloy Entertainment
1700 Broadway
New York, NY 10019
www.alloyentertainment.com

First edition July 2014

Cover design by Stephanie Mooney and Elaine Damasco
Cover photo © Gleb Semenjuk. Used under license from Shutterstock.com
Author photo © Dawn Fulwood

ISBN 978-1-939106-39-1 (ebook)
ISBN 978-1-939106-43-8 (paperback)

For a BMW 800 GS . . . and its rider.

CHAPTER ONE

EVERYONE IS EXACTLY like me.

There is no one like me.

I wrestle with these contradicting truths most nights while the others sleep. Tonight is worse because Marla has left me a note to see her in the morning. No one sees Marla and comes back. Lonnie reminded me of this after she snatched the note out of my shaking hand and read it for Ida, who promptly burst into tears. We didn't speak after that, lying in our bunks until lights out.

Above me, Lonnie steadily breathes in and out. She's not worrying herself out of a good night's sleep. She's not the one going to see Marla. Below me, Ida is quiet. I suspect she is awake, ruminating. She has a way of latching on to other people's stress and not letting go until everyone is happy again. I long to call out to her, but there is no talking in the dormitory after lights out.

The rough fabric of my cotton nightgown chafes so I lie very still. Once, during a training exercise, they gave me a satin blouse in place of my coarse uniform. For a few moments, I was completely *her*—eighteen-year-old Raven Rogen, my Authentic—down to the fabric. The slippery material felt like cool fingertips on a hot day. All I could think was: *She wears clothes like this every single day.*

I know everything about Raven and the world she lives in, thanks to the video footage I watch during my training sessions. But I have never experienced anything for myself—not even the sun. My entire life is an imitation of hers.

I am an Imitation.

All of us here are. From the time the tubes are removed and air is forced into our lungs, until our petri-grown organs learn to contract on their own, we are nothing but shadows of our Authentics. I used to think there was an Imitation for every Authentic, but when I asked my Examiner, Josephine, she laughed and said we'd need a whole lot more space here if that was the case. Only special Authentics get the privilege of a copy—ones with money, power, influence.

It seems as if there are thousands of us, though it's hard to tell exactly how many exist. Twig City is sorted into sections, our placement depending on our gender, how old we were when they "woke" us, and whether we've gotten a note from Marla. Those woken at a young age live in a different wing, where nurses and teachers chart their development daily. You have to be at least twelve to live on my floor—the training sector, where we learn to *become* our Authentic—but the oldest I've seen is somewhere around fifty. There is no saying how long you'll stay in this ward once you're here. Could be a week, could be a year, depending on when your Authentic needs you. I've been awake for five years. Training. Preparing. Waiting—for a note from Marla. And for what comes after.

Some say Marla is our creator—but I don't think so. I have a memory, a hazy nightmare, of the day I woke. None of the first faces I saw were female. One man in particular stands out in the fog. I can't recall his features, but the impression he left is one of utter fear. Though I can't explain it, I am positive this man is our creator.

Others say Marla is the gatekeeper. A walker between worlds, connecting us, the Imitations, to *them*. The humans, the womb-born, the Authentics.

I don't know which is true. All I know is no one ever returns from meeting with Marla.

Across the pitch-dark room comes a whisper, and I count down the seconds until an Overseer comes in. Overseers are the sentries, the silent guards who watch and wait, only intervening when a rule is broken or boundary overstepped. A minute later, I hear the sure, swift fall of an Overseer's feet as she makes her way to the offending bunk to bark an order of quiet at whoever it was. Probably Clora. She's new and headstrong. Lonnie speculates it is a trait from her Authentic. I hope not. If it's part of her DNA, it won't be easy an easy habit to break.

"This is your only warning," the Overseer threatens. "Another infraction and you'll be reported to Marla."

I'm convinced Overseers are paid to be cross. I've told this to my Examiner, Josephine, and she doesn't bother arguing so I know it's true. Josephine is more laid-back than most, but I've never told her the real truth: that the idea of leaving Twig City is terrifying. Instead, I tell Josephine what she wants to hear, what Imitations are supposed to say: When I am called to duty, I will be ready. I will serve my Authentic in any way necessary.

After all, I was created to serve.

The Overseer finishes her warning and exits the room, back to her monitoring booth full of cameras. I chase sleep, grazing my fingertips across its tail end but never fully catch it. Hours later, the lights come on, signaling to our windowless chamber that it is morning. I shove the blanket aside and sit up, blinking against a sea of sameness.

The sleeping room is a long rectangle with high ceilings and a bad echo, lined with triple-level bunk beds. Everyone here is part of a trio. Lonnie says it's because three's a crowd. It creates diversity and therefore animosity. It discourages the bonding that happens when there are only two. Ida tells her she's wrong because the three of us have bonded just fine. I see both points; no one else seems as close as we are, but no other trio has lasted this long. I've been with Lonnie and Ida since I began. Most others have lost at least one of their threesome to a note from Marla, only to have them replaced by a stranger.

And now I have a letter.

I slide out of my bunk and land lightly on my feet. In the bunk above, Lonnie is slow to wake, grumpily mumbling about coffee as she stretches her toned arms toward the ceiling. She thinks her Authentic must not be a morning person.

Ida stands more quickly. Her thick black hair ripples as she moves, mussed but manageable in its pixie cut. Her eyes are heavy and blinking but not from grogginess; her lids are puffy, rimmed in pink. The longer she stares at me, the more her bottom lip trembles. I slip my shoes on and fuss with my pale hair—anything to ignore Ida's nervous energy.

Anna, the girl whose bunk is closest to ours, catches my eye and nods. I nod back in silent hello. It is a daily ritual, simple and meaningless considering we never converse beyond this, but I will miss it when I'm gone.

While we wait for Lonnie, I take Ida's hand in mine and hold her palm open. Using my index finger, I trace the outline of a square and then a check mark inside it. *It's going to be okay,* I convey using our secret language. Ida takes my hand and scribbles a wavy line across my palm in return. A loose *W* for *whatever.*

I let my hand drop.

It started on paper, a shorthand code made up of symbols we'd exchange back and forth to communicate during lectures. When we got caught passing notes, we began drawing the pictures in invisible lines on each other's skin.

"Ven, I don't want you to go," Ida says in her soft voice, which always makes me think of dolls in pretty dresses. Porcelain. Breakable.

I don't acknowledge her plea. If she cries again, I fear I will, too.

"Time for breakfast," I say.

We fall into step together as the crowd of girls who live in this wing surge toward the breakfast hall. The air smells of sleepy bodies with an underlying chemical scent that drifts down from the pipes and mixes with everything, even the food and water.

Anna bumps my shoulder as she pushes past. I don't complain, because we're taught silence is best when there's nothing of value to say. Besides, the way to breakfast used to involve a lot more shoving and jostling for space. Notes from Marla have depleted our numbers.

We're the last group to arrive and the room, although large, is crowded. Four dormitories share this dining hall, a total of roughly two hundred forty women in plain uniforms.

Lonnie heads straight for the buffet line and taps her foot impatiently as she waits her turn. I wander to the coffee and muffins station with Ida and fill a plate even though my stomach feels packed with bricks.

As we sit down at our regular table, Lonnie glares suspiciously at Ida's plate. "Is that bran?"

"Bran's good for you," Ida says, her lips forming a pout.

I stare longingly at Lonnie's single piece of sausage and two small strips of bacon.

"Don't be too jealous," she says. "I had to sign up for an extra thirty minutes of cardio to get both."

As the smell hits me, it seems a small price to pay. I watch with rapture as she chews. She catches me looking. I force a bite of my muffin. "Yum," I say dryly.

"Maybe Ven will make Marla change her mind," Ida says abruptly.

Lonnie rolls her eyes and mumbles "not likely" around a mouthful of eggs.

Ida glares at her. "It's possible. Ven can be convincing when she wants to be."

"No one 'convinces' Marla," Lonnie says.

She's right. Even Ida knows it. "What do you think they want with you?" Ida asks quietly.

Lonnie and I share a look. There are only two reasons an Imitation gets a letter from Marla.

"They probably have an assignment for me," I say. Neither of us is willing to say the other option: that I'm wanted for harvesting. No one ever talks about it, but we all know it's the main reason we exist.

In training, we speak only of assignments. Missions. Most often, the job involves inserting yourself into the life of your Authentic when you're needed. For what, exactly, they don't say, and we've never been able to ask. Imitations who complete their assignments move from Training to Maintenance, where they get more free time than we have here. I've imagined hundreds of missions: giving speeches for a camera-shy Authentic; going to work while your Authentic goes on safari; walking the red carpet while your Authentic is sick in bed; being a surrogate mother . . .

"You're probably right that it's a mission," Ida says. "Something clandestine and exciting, I'm sure."

There is a note of forced cheerfulness in her voice. Anyone else listening would assume it was for my benefit, or Lonnie's, but I know better. Ida must convince herself there is no reason to panic.

"If you're really lucky, you'll get Relaxation," Lonnie suggests.

Relaxation is the ultimate reward, where you're sent when your Authentic is no longer in need of an Imitation. They say it's a hidden wing of Twig City full of nothing but leisure time. Sort of like retirement. Donuts and lounge chairs until our bodies give out. Exercise is no longer required six days a week and our food isn't rationed. Lonnie says that last part is too good to be true. Ida always rolls her eyes at that.

"That would mean my Authentic is dead," I point out.

"Not necessarily," Lonnie argues. "Maybe she just doesn't want an Imitation anymore."

"Or maybe she wants to meet you. Can you imagine that?

Living with humans? Pretending to be one of them?" Ida is far-away, her words wistful.

I force my hand steady and let Ida's comment pass without reply, choking down the smaller half of my muffin. I try to focus on my excitement rather than my fear. Because like it or not, I have a note to see Marla. And no one sees Marla and comes back.

CHAPTER TWO

AFTER BREAKFAST, THE three of us walk together behind the others to our designated changing room. The girls in our wing have ten minutes to report downstairs for physical activity. Our days are scheduled to the second in Twig City. This way, we don't have time to think about the fact that it's more like a prison than a city. No one says it out loud, but the absence of an exit is proof that it's true.

"Maybe you'll meet a hot guy," Lonnie says as we grab our gym uniforms from our cubbies.

"Maybe," I echo.

None of us have ever really interacted with boys. Twig City is segregated to prevent lasting relationships of that sort. Attachment is too complicated when you could get called up for duty at any time. To develop our social skills, we are treated to a quarterly mixer, where we are made to dress up and then marched upstairs to the boys' dormitory. For two hours, we are fed cookies and punch while static-filled music is cranked through the speakers. Once, a few couples tried dancing but as soon as their bodies made contact, the Overseers were there, pulling them apart and handing out punishment orders. No one dances anymore.

Ida turns her back to me as she quickly switches out her plain cotton sleep-shirt for the spandex material we are given to exercise in. She is one of the few girls with a penchant for modesty. The rest of us, either a result of living together for so long or our DNA programming, don't care.

I strip off my pajamas and yank my sports bra into place with sure movements while, across from me, Lonnie does the same. Both of our bodies are toned and lean but Lonnie's arms and calves are thicker than mine and her skin tone is more olive than my pale flesh and even paler white-blond hair. Molecular duplication at its finest. Ida's milky skin contrasts with the dark curtain of hair that ends halfway down her neck. I catch sight of a small scar I've never noticed before.

"What's that?" I ask, pointing to a spot just below her hairline.

"What's what?" Ida secures her sports bra and turns to me.

"The scar on your neck."

Lonnie and two other girls crowd in to look where I point. Ida strains but can't quite see it.

"I don't remember getting a cut there." Ida's brows scrunch with worry. She gives up trying to see the affected area and faces me instead.

"Why would she have a scar?" Lonnie asks, pushing through for a closer look.

"Maybe her Authentic got one and they had to match it," Clora offers.

No one says anything for a moment as we all contemplate

that. I don't say a word about the fact that I, too, have a small scar. On my forearm. Under bright lights, it's just barely visible on my translucent skin. I don't remember where mine came from, either.

"Girls, quit yappin' and get a move on," the Overseer near the door shouts, jolting me out of my thoughts.

The group disperses and the others shove their pajamas into hampers near the gym doors. A hand on my arm surprises me. It's Anna, watching me with hard eyes.

"You got a letter." It's not a question.

I wonder how she knows. I've only told Lonnie and Ida. Am I acting that differently?

Anna doesn't wait for me to answer. "What you've been told is wrong. Assignments, what happens after . . . it's not what they say."

My volume automatically lowers to match hers. I lean in. "What are you talking about? How do you know?"

She casts a quick look toward the door. Her words are rushed. "I can't explain. You have to trust me. Whatever you do, you can't let them send you to Relaxation. Okay?"

"But why—?"

Her chin juts. "Just promise me."

"Fine. I promise."

"Be careful, Ven."

Anna removes her hand from my arm and hurries past me into the gym. A few questioning stares point in our direction as the others join her. I am about to chase her down, to demand an answer, when a voice stops me short.

"Ven."

I turn and find Josephine waiting for me, her white uniform crisp and clean, her eyes patient and quiet like the rest of her. My heart jumps into my throat and pulses. "Yes?"

Her voice is soft. "I need you to come with me." My heart races.

This is it. Behind me, Ida gasps. The rest of the group flows around me, disappearing through the double doors.

"Marla?" I ask.

"Yes, but impromptu surveillance session first. Marla's orders." Josephine glances past me. "Do you need a moment?"

I nod in gratitude and walk to my friends.

Ida's face is pale beneath her dark hair. She throws herself against me, wrapping her arms around my neck. I hug her tight and kiss her hair. "It's going to be okay," I tell her in my best soothing voice. "I'll see you in Maintenance before we know it."

She nods against my shoulder, crying again. I want desperately to do the same. We both know nothing will be okay. I will quite possibly never see them again. But Ida lets me soothe her with my lies and I manage to hold it together for her sake. I murmur a few more empty reassurances before I gently break free of her hold.

I take her palm in mine once last time and trace a heart with my fingertip on her skin. "Love you, too," she murmurs, eyes swollen with moisture. I drop her hand and step back.

Then it's Lonnie's turn. We stare at each other for a long time. Her stoic expression and clenched jaw are stark reminders of Lonnie's personality. Her will to fight is automatic, an ingrained part of her. It is a trait that balances my quiet brooding and Ida's emotional outbursts. I've often wondered if we've been grouped together for this reason. As I stare at her, I imagine myself memorizing her strength so I can copy it later.

"Be brave," she says finally.

"I will," I promise.

That is all we say before she turns and drags Ida out the double doors. I stand and watch my friends vanish into the gym. Josephine hovers in the corner, waiting until I'm ready to usher me forward. My feet are heavy and it takes a moment to get them moving. Every step toward her feels like a step toward the end.

CHAPTER THREE

"JOSEPHINE, DO YOU know why I'm going?" I ask quietly as we navigate the maze of halls inside the women's wing of the City, making our way toward the monitoring room. It took me months after I woke to learn my way around the grid system of halls and residential wings. It's not difficult but it's large—and much is off-limits. I run my finger lightly along the steel of a door marked Do Not Enter in bold block letters. I've driven myself crazy wondering what lies in the prohibited areas. But not any more crazy than wondering what lies above and beyond the walls of this glorified warehouse I call home.

"No, I'm sorry, I . . . I really don't." The confusion in her tone indicates she's telling the truth. "Honestly, your letter was a surprise."

I cut my eyes toward her. "How do you mean?"

"Usually they tell me it's coming. So I can help you prepare. Most assignments are given a week or two's notice so we can use that time to prep you." Josephine hesitates and then says, "Impromptu surveillance sessions are not . . . common."

"I see," I mumble. I want to ask what reason they could possibly have for putting a rush order on me, but I hold back. Fear winds through me again as I recall Anna's warning: *What you've been told is wrong. Assignments, what happens after . . . it's not what they say.*

Not that they say much. Our only real window to the outside world is surveillance sessions. They are the most interesting and excruciating part of training. We're expected to study our Authentics and their world, to immerse ourselves and understand them so fully that, should we have to serve them, we will be ready at a moment's notice. The footage is always carefully edited, and so many times, I couldn't help but wonder what came after the cutoff.

All of Raven Rogen's recordings are shopping trips, parties, and luncheons with the rest of the city's socially elite young women. Raven is the shallowest Authentic I've ever seen. She graduated from an elite private school months ago and is taking a gap year before college to do "charity work," which mostly consists of buying tickets to fashion shows and galas for good causes. She doesn't seem to be making her way in the world so much as following a golden path someone—her father?—has laid out for her. Josephine has never shown me Raven's family, but I know her father is well-off, involved in politics and nonprofits, and he expects her to be the face of the family. She's never mentioned a mother.

Last week, Raven had lunch with the visiting French ambassador and his wife as a representative of a charity board she serves on. The entire meal was small talk and comparing cultures in the small, clueless way only Raven can.

"Are French fries really made in France?" Raven had asked while batting coated lashes at the Frenchman. The ambassador's wife had stared ahead with a half-curled lip while the two of them flirted right in front of her.

I cringed but watched while Josephine quizzed me on the intricacies of foreign policy and made me mimic my Authentic's etiquette.

As soon as the ambassador and his wife left, Raven's suggestive smile faded and she stopped flipping her hair, instead scanning the restaurant with sharp eyes. After a few moments, her gaze landed on whomever she'd been looking for, and her entire face lit with excitement and something else I couldn't read. I'd never seen her look at anyone like that before. The newcomer came into view and I caught sight of a broad shoulder in a white button-down shirt before everything went black.

Sometimes, Raven's videos feel like study guides with only partial answers.

When we reach the monitoring room, Josephine closes the door behind us. The room is small, no more than eight feet across in any direction, and completely lined with monitors. There is a chair in the corner, but I never use it. Instead, I place myself in the center where I can best view all the screens—and where I can practice moving like Raven as I study her. It comes easily to me, impersonating the person I was built to mimic. I wonder if it's like this for everyone, but we're forbidden from talking about it with the others. They say it's for our privacy but I suspect it's for our Authentics'.

Josephine hits a button on a remote and the monitors snap to life with flashes of color. I stare, wide-eyed and unmoving, at a busy street. Dark-painted sedans roll past stores with sidewalk displays and bored-looking valets. She's probably shopping. Again.

Across the steady stream of traffic, I recognize the navy blue window coverings and wrought-iron café tables at Mia's, a small Mediterranean café Raven often goes to for brunch and espresso. Two doors down is Renwick Gallery. Raven attended an opening there last week where she spent the better part of the evening flirting with the CEO of ExRon Petroleum. She left with promises of a trip for two to Crete next summer and smudged lipstick at the corners of her mouth.

The camera—a tiny device I suspect is fastened to one of Raven's security guards—swings from the street to the sidewalk, revealing an ocean of foot traffic. High-heeled women carrying leather handbags and mobile devices hurry by, all breathtakingly different and beautiful. The sounds of blaring horns and raised voices fill the speakers. A rushed energy leaks out of the monitors, electrifying the air around me. For one moment, I close my eye and pretend it's me out there, free, alive. Human.

"Ven," Josephine says warningly, reminding me that she is still here—and that I'm not out there. Not yet.

Opening my eyes, I scan the screens for my Authentic. At first, there's nothing, but then I notice a familiar face stepping out of a shiny black car at the curb. The door is held by a driver I don't recognize but that doesn't mean anything. The Rogens change employees like they change clothes.

"I'm telling you, that sketchy-looking bum was following us on his bicycle. He was staring right at us," says the blond beauty I recognize as Raven's best friend, Taylor Douglas. Her delicate features are a sharp contrast to her lethal tongue. I know from watching that she is just as quick to insult as she is to smile. Usually, she does both simultaneously. But never to Raven. Her barbs are loaded, but always just shy of mean.

"You're being paranoid. No one's following us." The voice comes from inside the car, but it's her. I know it's her because sometimes it feels as if it's me. A different, more uncaring version of me. Raven's tone lacks Taylor's bite, but that's only because she's with her own kind. I've seen how she treats those she views as inferior. It's the only time I stumble in my impersonation.

Taylor steps aside and a slender girl of eighteen emerges from the car. Her blond hair is swept away from her face. Striking blue eyes are lightly lined and expertly made-up to look captivating and cosmetic-free—a feat that takes her an hour on a good day. She and Taylor stand eye to eye but only because Raven's wearing taller heels today. She is graceful and lithe and completely sure of herself as she runs a hand over her skirt and blouse. The fabric and design is unmistakably Jorge Estrada, a shop the two of them frequent often. Not a wrinkle or glitch exists in her ensemble but Raven adjusts and smoothes it anyway. Habit.

And because her habits must become mine, I run a hand over my thighs.

Staring at Raven is always both jolting and fascinating. I'm not quite her twin. More like a carbon copy. Same watermark. Same DNA stamping. But she got all the upgrades.

"Besides, the windows are tinted, Tay. He couldn't have been staring at us," Raven adds, slipping her arm through Taylor's as they start down the sidewalk.

"Well, he was gross."

Raven's brows lift. "Gross like Lucas Snidd? Because you didn't seem to have a problem when you two—"

"Eww. Okay, stop." Taylor shakes her head, her golden locks swishing around her face. Raven laughs, but it's abrasive and lacking humor. "It was a political move. You wouldn't understand."

"Are you implying I don't understand politics, or that I refuse to sleep my way to the top?" Raven asks.

Taylor smirks. "Both." Raven opens her mouth to say something but Taylor cuts her off. "And don't be a prude. There's nothing wrong with using sex as a means to an end. Especially if that end is becoming the ruler of the free world."

Raven stares at Taylor for a moment, eyes wide and reproachful. I do the same, careful to match my lifted brows to hers. "Good luck with that. There's never been a woman president," Raven reminds her.

Taylor grins. "Not yet. But the general public has yet to be exposed to the brilliance that is Taylor Douglas." She waves a hand over herself in a flourish.

Raven chuckles, the tension broken. "I'm so glad we're taking our gap year together," she says.

Except that Taylor is actually doing something with her gap year—interning at campaign offices around DC during election season—while Raven spends her time ordering her household staff around.

They continue to walk, the other pedestrians keeping a respectful distance. Raven falls silent, chewing her lip. "I'm sorry I brought Lucas up; I—"

"Oh, I don't care about that." Taylor waves a dismissive hand and suddenly stops to point at a display in a shop window. "Look!"

Shoulder to shoulder, they pause to admire a mannequin in the glass front of a costume shop. The corset is the only piece of real clothing and it has only two full inches of actual fabric; the rest is revealing black lace. A black feather boa embossed with red rhinestones is draped around the headless neck. The heels strapped to the plastic, webbed feet lift the entire monstrosity at least six inches off the pedestal. I am horrified. The girls seem mesmerized.

"Amazing," Raven breathes.

"Amazing," I repeat, if only to show Josephine I'm paying attention instead of imagining having to wear this scandalous scrap of material for one of Raven's admirers.

They turn away and the camera zooms out, capturing the ripple of the crowd parting for them. Eyes of passersby flit up and away before they can rest openly on either of the girls' faces. Power. It emanates from both of them, despite their youth. Or perhaps because of it.

A few yards back, two middle-aged men in black-on-black uniforms shadow the girls, trying but failing miserably to blend. Raven's security is almost as tight out there as mine is in here. Taylor reaches into her purse, and pulls out a wallet from a side pocket. "Lattes on me?"

"You don't have to ask me twice," Raven says.

As they round the corner, an arm shoots out, catching Taylor by the shoulder and shoving her away. Shrieking, she spins out of view before I can tell whether she falls. The hooded assailant steps up to Raven and grabs her wrist. She screams, but it's lost in the scuffling of boots as her security team rushes forward and pries the stranger's hand away.

Raven stumbles back. There is a grunt and a shot is fired, but I can't tell where it came from. I flinch as someone exhales in a growling yell. One of the security guards crumples awkwardly to the ground in front of whoever is wearing the camera and yells, "Run!" But before he can escape, the person wearing the camera doubles over with a grunt. From my tilted view of the sidewalk I watch Raven's black heels, followed closely by two sets of scuffed boots, scurry toward a set of wheels parked at the curb. There is another shout, the camera jolts, and the screen goes black.

My knees buckle and fear winds through my gut. My mind reels with the possibilities of what happened to Raven. Did she escape? Was she shot? Does she need an organ? Or worse?

"Is she—?" is all I can manage, Anna's warning echoing in my head. *Whatever you do, you can't let them send you to Relaxation.*

"She's not dead," Josephine quickly interjects, gesturing for me to take a seat. I fall into it heavily as she rolls her chair in front of mine.

"What happened?" I press. The chaos of those fifteen seconds threatens to paralyze me.

Her jaw is firmly set and her normally warm brown eyes are distant, intent on the task. "There was an attack."

"An attack," I repeat, trying to understand. We've never been shown much in the way of violence. My heart races. Cold moisture coats my palms.

"Some men tried to assault Raven. She escaped. I'm sorry, but that's all I know."

Normally, after a session, there is a period of debriefing where Josephine is allowed to fill in some of the blanks for me, but lately, she's been limited with her explanations. Today, it seems, there are none.

"Oh," I say into the quiet.

Josephine fiddles with the delicate gold necklace hanging from her neck, the letter *Z* stamped into its circular pendant. I wonder what it stands for. I've known her for what consists of my entire life. But the truth is, I know nothing about her. Nothing of value anyway.

"I need to do one last check before you go," she says, breaking the weighted silence. "You up for that?"

I nod.

"Okay, let's begin. Full name?"

"Raven Celeste Rogen."

"Address?"

I falter for a moment. I haven't had to recall this one for some time now. "Eighteen-hundred H Street. Washington, DC."

"Good." Josephine makes a note on her clipboard. "Hobbies?"

"Shopping and charity work," I say, trying to hold back an eye roll. Raven's scales are tipped in one direction and it's not in service to the less fortunate.

Josephine looks up at me. "How do you feel?" she asks gently.

I try to imagine myself as Raven, adopting confidence, pretending to be someone with an innate sense of control. What would they say if they knew I was dreading the thing they'd created me for?

But I square my shoulders and tell her exactly what she wants to hear. "I am eager to serve."

She nods. "Then you are ready to see Marla."

CHAPTER FOUR

JOSEPHINE TAKES ME through a series of halls I've never seen. The low, vibrating hum is the same in this wing, but oddly, there are no pipes above. Instead, scrubbed white ceiling tiles contain vents that blow cool air over me. It's an entirely different sensation from the filtered air we get below, and goose bumps break out along my arms.

I haven't even left the building and already I'm in foreign territory.

The way ahead is blocked by a door with a large red *X*. Josephine stops and produces a plastic keycard.

"This is as far as I go," she says.

I nod and swallow hard, averting my eyes to hide my uncertainty.

"You'll be fine," she adds. "You are very good at your role, Ven. You have nothing to worry about."

A moment of silence passes as I search for a way to say good-bye. A peek at Josephine's face shows she's just as lost as I am. She puts her hand on my shoulder. It's touching, this small proof of her affection.

"You'll go through this door, and then check in at the desk."
Josephine clears her throat and presses her lips together in a tight
almost-smile. She fingers her pendant absently. "Perhaps we'll see
each other again."

I jerk my head up, my eyes narrowing and shrewd. "You
think so?"

Josephine's smile fades. "Sure. Better get going now."

She swipes her card along a small black panel and something
clicks inside the door. It opens automatically, a yawning mouth
waiting to consume me. An alternate universe intent on whisking
me away.

"Good luck, *Raven*," Josephine says just as the door closes
between us.

The room in front of me is square and windowless, with an
oversized desk in one corner. The middle-aged woman behind it
is familiar. Estelle. I've seen her making announcements in assem-
blies and it is her nasally voice we hear on the intercom when
there is news to be dispatched to Twig City.

"Can I help you?" She smiles, her lips pushing dimples to her
cheeks.

There is something wonderfully other about her. Authentic.
Human. I can sense it on her and on Josephine in the same way I
can feel it missing from me.

"Marla sent for me," I say, my throat dry.

I produce the note from my pocket and hand it over. Estelle
slips on a pair of glasses that look too small to be of real help and
squints at the paper. The barely legible scrawl matches that of
another note on the desk and I wonder who else has been called
up today.

Estelle nods. "Ah, yes. Ven. We're expecting you. Please have a seat. Marla will be right with you." She motions for me to sit in one of six blue-cushioned chairs along the wall. They're all empty. I sink into the one on the far left as Estelle scurries out of sight. Around the corner, a door opens. I hear voices and then nothing as the door shuts again. I cross my legs, trying to get comfortable, and then immediately uncross them. We were taught early on that our bodies are fragile, something to be protected and cared for, and leg-crossing cuts off circulation. I have a bad habit of doing it when I'm anxious.

A moment later, Estelle reappears. "Follow me, please," she says.

She turns on her heel and leads me down another hallway to a door guarded on either side by two men in dark suits. They stand, arms crossed, eyes locked on something faraway and invisible to everyone but them. They don't move as I approach, and it occurs to me that I'm invisible to them. I'm already a ghost.

Marla rises as I enter the room. The effort of heaving herself upright seems to drain her of oxygen. She leans with both palms on the desk, pushing herself to her full height, her dark hair a triangle around her flushed face.

I've seen her only once before. She gave a speech to the entire women's population last year, something encouraging about our roles being vital to the betterment of society. We sat in the back and Lonnie slept through it. The speech came on the heels of an Imitation having a breakdown in the lunchroom. They'd discontinued serving some brand of tea and she'd dissolved into a fit of screams and sobs about how they were oppressing her individuality. They dragged her out . . . and we never saw her again.

Lonnie said the girl was brave. Ida said she was stupid. I didn't say anything.

By the time I've crossed the room to stand in front of Marla, she is winded. Her ample chest swells and retracts a dozen times before she speaks to me.

"Who are you?" she huffs.

I blink. Didn't Estelle tell—?

"Go on," she says, louder now. "What is your name? Your *real* name."

And then I realize what game we're playing. "Hello. My name is Raven Rogen. And you are . . . ?" I say, adding a trace of condescension to my voice.

"Not bad." Marla eyes me, lips pursed. "Thank you for coming."

I can't bring myself to say, "You're welcome." We both know I didn't have a choice in the matter.

"Have a seat," she adds.

We both sit. I clasp my hands together in my lap to keep them still.

The room is large. The walls may have been lavender once, but they've faded into a dirty fog. A bookcase along one wall brims with hardback manuals, and behind the desk hangs a giant tapestry that looks like some sort of flag. Near the ceiling rests a single filthy window, too high for any sort of view. What a waste to have a window in this crossroads, where no one is ever in a mood to enjoy a rare glimpse of sunlight.

Marla is staring intently at a stack of papers on her desk. She makes clucking noises while she reads. I try to decipher my fate based on the sounds.

Finally, she looks up at me. "*Raven*," she says, setting the papers down and placing her hands over them. "I'm sure it comes as no surprise that you're needed for an assignment."

My heart seizes, skips three beats, then starts again. Marla is waiting for me to speak. "Mmm," I say without opening my lips.

"Something has happened with your Authentic."

I sit quietly, incapable of sound or response. Raven was injured after all. Organ harvesting. It's everything I dread. I am finished.

A full thirty seconds pass before I manage a nod. It seems to be all Marla needs.

"Now," she says. "There is a car waiting outside. The men in the hall will escort you. Usually, we take more time to brief you, to prepare you for the outside. I realize much of this will come as a shock. This is all very last minute, due to the sensitive nature of the circumstances."

"The circumstances being . . . ?" My voice trails off.

"That your Authentic needs you, of course." She picks up her papers again, as if that explains everything.

"Is she hurt? Was she shot?"

Marla frowns, unused to being questioned. "No. She's not hurt."

"Kidnapped, then?" I press.

"Everything will be explained when you reach your location. You've been requested and that is all you need to know for now." She says this with such a heavy dose of reproach that the rest of my questions wither on my tongue. I know enough. If Raven's not hurt, then she's not lying on a gurney in need of my liver or spleen. This is not harvesting, and it's not Relaxation.

Yet.

"Stand up and let me see you, then," she says, sighing as she rises with me. It feels as if I've already disappointed her somehow. I step away from my chair, arms at my sides, as Marla inspects me.

"Good Lord Almighty, why didn't they dress you properly?" she mutters.

I glance down at my gym clothes. "Josephine didn't—"

"Never mind about that. You'll change when you get there. Gentlemen!" Marla calls. "The door!"

The door opens and the two men from the hall file into the office. One stands at the back while the other man walks to the curtain behind Marla's chair and pulls it aside.

Behind it stands a narrow door, painted the exact same shade as the wall and almost unnoticeable even without the tapestry obscuring it. Knowing it leads outside sends a thrill of sick antici-pation through me; just how many of us have passed through this doorway and never returned?

"Due to the clandestine nature of your assignment, we must be discreet about your exit," Marla says. *Clandestine.* Ida would be thrilled.

I rise, wondering briefly what exit they would have offered me had my departure not required discretion. I follow Marla through the narrow passage, careful not to touch the grimy walls on either side. Mold and various other plant life dots the walls, a mixture of building material and earth.

The walk is short, and soon the walls give way to a metal door held open by security man number one. The air coming through the door smells different from what I know—cleaner, no chemi-cals. I don't have more than a second to think about how my feet have crossed the threshold and I am standing outside—*outside!*—when Marla barks: "Ven, this way."

She stands beside a sleek black car that hums quietly in the alley, its nose pointed at the exit. I recognize it immediately as the car from the footage, Raven's car, and realize these are Raven's guards.

One of the men opens the door and stands aside for me to climb in. Marla stops me, a hand on my arm that is quickly removed. Her expression tightens and she eyes the area where her fingers landed, as if she didn't mean to actually touch me.

"This is where we part ways," she says. "Good luck."

"You're not coming?" Panic consumes me; the last familiar face I know is about to vanish. Even though it's Marla, I want to latch on to her like she's a safety net. These men, this car, whatever lies beyond—all of it is foreign. I bite the inside of my cheek and channel Lonnie. *Be brave.*

Marla shakes her head, oblivious to my unease. "You don't need me. You've trained for this for years." She ushers me into the car, and before I can think of a single thing to say, she is gone.

Inside the car, the leather is warm underneath my touch. I've been inside a car once before, as a training exercise. They called it "human experience." An Overseer drove around the track they'd constructed in the canvas-covered gym area. While all the other kids stared out the window or down at the belt strapping them in, I kept tabs on the dashboard. The controls and dials were fascinating; all that potential for speed. But the speedometer didn't pass thirty before Ida's face turned green. We all had to scramble out before she threw up on us.

In this car, a dark partition blocks my view of the dashboard.

I can barely make out the faces of my two escorts as they stare ahead, expressionless, hidden behind their impenetrable glasses. Raven always ignores them, so I do, too.

We ease forward, slowly at first. We pass out of the alley, the road widening. To my left, Twig City rises up, a massive gray shape I don't recognize, having only experienced it from the inside.

A metal sculpture of a tree decorates one side of the building, its thick trunk and barren branches glinting in the dappled sunlight. Rusted lettering runs the length of it, but the car picks up speed before I have a chance to make out more than CORP. And then, a moment later, obscured behind a wall of real trees, the only home I've ever known disappears.

CHAPTER FIVE

AN HOUR LATER, my fingers are stiff from clutching the edge of the leather seat as the car races down the highway. At this speed, I'm sure a crash would be fatal. Outside the windows, the ground is eaten up beneath our tires and the world spins by in a blur: open fields. Faded grass with hacked-off edges. Trees with brown or golden leaves clinging to their gnarled armlike branches, the harbingers of swift-approaching winter.

I've seen enough footage to recognize mid-October as autumn. Most Authentics grumble about the cold. But seeing it for the first time in the real world, nature's barrenness is oddly beautiful.

The driver hits his blinker and we turn onto a bridge, the car bouncing and the tires groaning against the grooved metal. The river rushes beneath us, frothing white where the water slams over rocks. The stilted pylons that hold us up above the water's surface amaze me. I've read about bridges but never saw one on a training video. Raven rarely leaves the city.

After a while, the open fields give way to squared-off walls and decayed buildings with boarded-up windows. They are old. Unkempt. Trash litters the gutters: old wrappers, smashed cups, and even what looks like the flattened remains of a squirrel. Street signs are missing letters or have been painted over. The few remaining sport a single letter: *M* or *K* or *L*.

The car slows, and I wonder why we're stopping here. But then I see the reason for our pause: Authentics. A pair of men with scraggly beards has stepped into the street, unconcerned with the car bearing down on them.

I am completely caught up by the sight. Their clothes—rags even by Twig City standards—suggest they've been worn far more than they've been washed. And the hollow look in their eyes is shocking. Authentics are so much more than we are—more feeling, more depth, more life. And yet these people look dead inside. Where were they on my video footage? Certainly not a part of Raven's world.

My driver hits his horn to hurry them along, but they just turn to glare before ambling slowly forward. Finally, the way is clear and the car takes off, not stopping again until we reach what is obviously a nicer part of town. Windows are made from glass instead of covered in scuffed planks. Pedestrians, not debris, glut the walkways. The people here look cleaner, well kept. Alive. They wear bright hats and walk tiny dogs on thin leashes, pausing in front of storefront displays. These Authentics keep completely to themselves while managing to look disdainfully at everything around them.

We move through a pattern of red and green traffic lights, passing grassy lawns manicured to perfection. An elongated pool reflects a singular pointed statue rising high into the sky on the far end—the Washington Monument, something I've only ever experienced through a two-dimensional screen. My nose brushes the window as I stare at the perfect glass-like surface of the water until it passes out of sight.

We don't slow again until we pull into an alleyway so narrow I worry the sides of the car will be scraped off. No one speaks when the car stops. The driver gets out and disappears through a side door into the building on our left. The other man stays with me, and I fidget, twisting my fingers together while we wait in silence. My stomach knots and unknots until it is a rhythm I can predict with precision. *One, two, three, knot. One, two, three, loosen.*

I count through it eleven more times before our driver returns. Beside him is a gray-haired man with a square jaw and a broad chest. He comes straight to my door and pulls it open, peering in at me.

"Hello, Raven," he says.

"H-hello." My throat is dry.

He reaches in and, gingerly, I place my hand against his and allow him to pull me to my feet outside the car. Ahead, the alley narrows until it dead-ends in a cluster of green Dumpsters. Above, a massive tower looms black as night, taller than I would have thought possible. Twisted metal runs the length of both sides, like steel pythons trying to squeeze the life out of the building. The men approach it comfortably. This must be it. My new home.

"This way," says the gray-haired leader.

He ushers me through a side door into a lobby cut out of granite, with smooth, onyx-colored walls. In the center of the room is a cluster of lush trees, branches dripping with tiny pink cherry blossoms. Their sweet scent permeates the space, making the air seem fuller despite our foursome being the lobby's only occupants. To my left, the main entrance leads in from the street front. Large cutout windows frame a revolving glass door that spins on its own. A doorman, his figure shadowed through the tinted glass, stands just outside. He tips his hat to people who pass by. No one acknowledges him in return.

My escort clears his throat. His brows are drawn in a look of impatience. I hurry, concentrating on planting one foot in front of the other, willing my heart to slow to something more rhythmic, less like a heart attack. I have no idea what awaits here, but I think it can't be good, or everyone wouldn't be so god-awful serious about it.

At the far end of the lobby is a single elevator compartment. Once inside, I catch sight of my reflection in the chrome doors. My white-blond hair is disheveled and wild. My skin is paler than usual, but what startles me are my eyes. They are wider than I've ever seen, full of cobalt electricity. In the distorted reflection they appear glassy with shock. I try to smooth out my horrified expression, but then the car shoves upward and I hang tight to the railing behind me, pretending my stomach isn't in my throat. Watching someone ride an elevator isn't the same as experiencing it.

A chime dings, and the yellow light above the door announces we are at the uppermost level, the penthouse. My nausea settles slightly now that the elevator has stopped. The doors open and the three men hover close behind me, effectively shoving me out.

The hallway is bright—too bright after the dimness of the car and the elevator. I blink furiously and keep my chin down, my hair creating a curtain between me and whatever is waiting. Beneath my feet is a carpet so plush that I am certain my toes would disappear into the thick threads if I removed my shoes. In Twig City, the only carpet is the flat lime-green stuff in the shower area. It's scratchy underfoot and smells of mold. I never walk barefoot there if I can help it.

We leave the hall and enter a room on the right. Nerves, excitement, fear; a thousand different emotions dance across the pulse of my heartbeat. My breath quickens as they merge into one giant panic.

I sense his presence before I see him. Goose bumps break out along my neck and trail down my back. Directly in front of an ornate brick fireplace stands a man. Slight and bald, his head shines like the granite walls in the lobby. I think if I catch just the right angle, I will see my own reflection in his cranium. A hysterical laugh bubbles inside me, lodging in my chest and sticking there. I cannot laugh. Not now.

The man clears his throat and nods at me. "Welcome, Raven."

A tremor of fear runs through my insides at the sound of his voice. A picture flashes in my mind, too hazy to be remembered.

The man sighs. "Stand up straight."

I do as he asks, raising my head and letting my hair swing away from my face. At full height, I'm only an inch or two shorter than he is. He is surprisingly average in stature considering the fear he evokes with the mere sound of his voice.

"Do you speak coherently or do we manufacture them mute now?" he asks sharply.

"I speak very well, sir," I say. My voice is small. I feel like Ida.

"Good damn thing." He lets out a short laugh. "Would've been ironic, me of all people getting a defective piece of equipment." There is familiarity in his expression, an intimacy between himself and the "equipment" he speaks of.

And just like that, something inside my memory unlocks. Nameless faces, the edges of their white lab coats glinting underneath fluorescent lights. Their eyes clinical as they poke and prod and test for things beyond my comprehension. One face in particular, an orb of pale flesh from chin to crown. Shrewd eyes devoid of warmth or welcome to the world I'd woken into. He never spoke directly to me that day but I heard his voice clear enough; he'd barked the order to move me into the training ward as soon as my rubbery legs could take me there.

Standing here before me in this posh penthouse, he's traded his lab coat for a designer suit but the eyes and voice are the same. I know for certain who he is. He's the man I saw when I opened my eyes for the first time.

He is my creator.

CHAPTER SIX

"ARE YOU FEELING all right?" The man watches me.

He made me. This man standing before me molded me with his very own hands. I should be elated or grateful or at least curious about the Authentic responsible for giving me life—but I'm not. He is the monster from my nightmares.

"It's been an eventful day," I manage to say.

Everything about him is so precise, even his jacket lapel doesn't stretch as he neatly tucks his arms behind his back. "Yes, well, I'm sure this is more excitement than you're used to, but you'd do well to acclimate quickly. Things move much faster here than they do in Twig City. I trust you can keep up?"

"Yes, sir." It's nothing more than a whisper but he nods. It's good enough.

"The staff, with the exception of Gus here—" as he gestures to the gray-haired man who escorted me, a gold ring glints on his middle finger "—believes you to be my daughter, Raven. You will act accordingly, even within the privacy of your new home."

"Yes, sir," I mumble again.

He throws a glance over my shoulder at Gus and barks, "Leave us."

My heart bangs against my chest like a kettledrum.

He doesn't speak again until we're alone.

"My name is Titus Rogen, but you will call me 'Father.' Do you understand?"

I nod. He is so close, my nose almost brushes his.

"There is a lot to go over but first and foremost, you are here because there is a threat against my daughter, your Authentic. Several attempts have been made on her life and while none have been successful in mortally harming her, we have yet to bring her assailants to justice. Until the threat is neutralized, you will be her. You will walk, talk, and act like her. You will attend all of her functions and fulfill all of her obligations. You'll get up to speed immediately and then we will begin the process of drawing them out. Your success in the mission will be defined by how well you perform as a target."

"You want them to *attack* me?" I gasp.

There is absolutely no apology whatsoever in him as he answers. "Yes. I want them alive but I'll take them however I can get them."

I say nothing as the full weight of my assignment sinks in. This is no heart transplant, but it's also no adventure. No clandestine glamour. No pretense of family. Lonnie would be so pissed right now. And Ida . . . Ida would crumble into ash.

My creator—my new father—is already moving on. "I know you go by Ven in Twig City. That will not be tolerated here. Henceforth, your name is Raven Rogen and you will only answer to that name. Am I clear?"

There is a pause and then his expression contorts. "Child?" he snaps, clearly losing patience.

I nod a second time and manage, "Yes, sir."

"Good. 'Sir' is fine. 'Father' is better." He watches me, waiting.

"Father." I shove the word out of my mouth. I feel funny for saying it, not just to him, but to anyone. Imitations don't have mothers and fathers. We don't have family. We just are.

My creator should know this better than anyone.

The tension drains from his shoulders. He steps back and gestures to the furniture. "We need to discuss this arrangement if it's to work out. Sit."

I lower myself to a leather couch.

"First, Rogen Tower is your home now. You can go anywhere you like except my private offices. Those are off-limits, even to my daughter."

"Where is she? Your daughter?" I ask before I can stop myself.

His eyes harden. "You do not get to ask me questions," he snaps. "I would like this arrangement to be mutually beneficial. For that to happen, there are certain rules that must be followed. Boundaries, if you will."

"Mutually beneficial?" I echo.

"I get to end the threat against my daughter and you get to experience life as it exists in the outside world. For however long your experience here lasts," he adds.

I can only stare at him. Did he really just say that my payment for dying is to sleep in a nice bed?

"I must say, you're off to a rather slow start."

His words do the trick and I realize that I'm failing at the one thing they created me for. As a trained Imitation, I should show more initiative, a willingness to integrate myself as Raven Rogen and do what I can to eliminate the danger against her. It's what I was made to do. To be an obedient Imitation, it shouldn't matter that my assignment is to allow myself to be threatened and quite possibly attacked.

"I apologize. It's a lot to take in. Marla didn't give me much to go on before I left."

He frowns. "You've seen the footage in your training?"

"Yes, but it was limited."

"Limited how?"

"It mainly showed clips of Raven shopping or eating or attending parties."

Titus smiles, an expression somewhere between smug and condescending. "Was there so much missing that you weren't prepared to sit in my living room and take instruction on how to shop and eat and attend parties?"

I lift my chin. "Yes, sir. I mean, no, sir. I can handle it just fine."

"Good. As for the footage provided, you saw what you needed to see. The rest is here." From the small table near the window, he retrieves a rectangular tablet and offers it to me. I swipe the screen with my index finger and it springs to life in vivid, inter-active color.

"The spreadsheets and picture albums are divided into cat-egories. 'Home,' 'Social,' and 'Hobbies.' You will need to famil-iarize yourself with every face, location, and activity in each one. Start with 'Home.' It will give you a list of employees and a floor plan for the house. Your daily routine is also loaded, including a strict exercise regimen. Training doesn't stop just because you're in the field."

I swipe through a few pages of household information. Titus lives in the penthouse apartment of Rogen Tower, which is comprised of two floors: a lower one where I currently sit, complete with a living space, a kitchen, offices, bedrooms, and a library. A room near the entrance is marked with the words Off-Limits. So are the entire west wing and the stairwell.

The upper level has a gym, swimming pool, and roof deck and is only accessible from an elevator located in the back of the suite. So far, fresh air and sunshine might be the only redeeming aspect of my assignment.

"Study this and get up to speed. Tomorrow you start her routine. I don't think I need to tell you how *disastrous* it would be if someone discovered who and what you really are. And that includes the rest of my staff. Do we have an understanding?"

I nod.

"I cannot hear your head rattle," he says wryly.

I clutch the tablet to my chest. "I'll study this tonight and be ready to go first thing in the morning."

"And you will carry out your orders until there are no orders left to execute?"

"I was created to serve, Father." Every word is a jab in my gut but I manage to spit it out.

"Excellent. Gus!" Titus shouts, and I jump.

"Boss?" a gruff voice says behind me.

"Show Raven to her room."

"Yes, sir."

Titus looks at me once more, then leaves through a side door.

It shuts behind him before I can see where it leads. He is gone and, for the moment, I can breathe again.

I turn to Gus. He waits for me, an impatient expression on his already scowling face. "Come on, then," he says.

We take the curving hallway until we reach a blue door. He turns the knob and shoves it inward, flicking a switch before stepping aside. I stop and stare at my new accommodations. I've never seen anything so luxurious, and it takes me a full minute to realize it is meant for me alone.

The bedroom is almost as big as the entire sleeping room back in Twig City—a space that holds twenty bunks for sixty girls. There are no fluorescent lights here, no pipes humming with power. The sleeping room in Twig City is drafty and above all, loud. Other than my own intake of breath and Gus's impatient huffing, there is no sound here.

Inside, there's the same plush carpeting as the hall, though here it's the color of honey—a sticky treat I've had on toast exactly twice in my whole existence. I think it is my favorite food but I can't know for sure. The thick rug sweeps in all directions, uninterrupted until it disappears underneath a four-poster bed. The furniture is similarly colored and cut, a matching suite. Above me, illuminating the entire space, is a chandelier dripping with crystals.

"Someone will come get you in the morning. Sleep well." Gus shuts the door and there is a click as a lock is turned from the outside, trapping me in the room.

The second I am alone, I flop on the feather bed and stare up at the ceiling, so unlike the loud, pipe-laden one above my bunk in Twig City. It occurs to me that I will sleep in a room alone for the first time since I awoke from the incubator. There is no Lonnie above or Ida below to whisper with before lights out, giggling about the sad way the female librarian stares at the thin-haired janitor or daydreaming about what it would be like to live on the outside.

In all our musings about missions, we never imagined a scenario like this. But the stark reality of mine is clear.

I am bait, pure and simple.

I will be lucky to get out alive.

CHAPTER SEVEN

THE MORNING COMES too fast. I'd expected to lay awake all night, tortured by the knowledge that this night spent on silk sheets could be my first and last. Instead I succumbed to the luxury and dreamed of a life where honey wasn't rationed and daily cardio was optional. A world where Twig City didn't exist, its residents scattered and matriculated into Authentic society. The idea is so far-fetched it takes me a moment to come all the way back to my own reality.

As soon as the light streams in through the curtains, I sit up and grab the tablet. Titus said to start with the household staff, but I skip to Raven's friends, curious about the people I've seen during surveillance sessions. Taylor Douglas is first. The entry contains a photo of her along with a short bio: *Daughter of a politician, rich. Party girl. Graduated top of class. Politically ambitious.*

The last line makes me snort. Ambitious is an understatement. This girl is on the twenty-five-year plan, right into the White House. The next face catches my eye and I read through the description. *Lacey Hawthorne: Freshman at Georgetown.*

General Studies. Daughter of Police Chief. Charities include: SPCA, Homeless America, Wounded Warrior Project.

I recognize the pretty, dark-skinned girl from Raven's group of friends. Lacey's the lowest on the social ladder that makes up Raven's inner circle. Not because of money or power but because she lacks their venom. It's made her the butt of more than one of their jokes. Through the years of footage, I've watched their ribbing change her into someone she wasn't always—someone harder, more ruthless. Cunning.

I flip to another. Brenna Strong. Raven's second best friend. Freckles dot her nose and cheeks, their shade of brown almost an exact match to her hair and eyes. Her smile is deceptively soft. *Daughter of a federal judge. Interns part-time for a gay-lesbian lobbyist group. Charities include: Brazilian-American Awareness Foundation and Heels for the Hungry.*

What I know, and what it doesn't say, is this girl is almost as lethal as Taylor.

I think back to the video footage from a day when Brenna and Raven got drunk on the judge's private Scotch, and Brenna ranted about Lacey's inability to think for herself. When Lacey found out about it, she let herself get caught with Brenna's boyfriend.

Behind their backs, Taylor and Raven call these two the West End Witches.

My fingers swipe faster and farther, past handsome boys with names like Daniel and Caine, into the grown-up politicians that populate Raven's world of parties and benefit galas. A short intro section advises me to pay close attention to the notations underneath the names. Many of them are direct benefactors of Titus's generous campaign contributions. The faces are listed in priority order.

The first is Senator Ryan. *Second term in office. Political platform includes: Science and Research, City Economic Segregation Bill, Social Classification System. Wife deceased (myeloma). One son: Daniel.*

I swipe backward to the friend section and find Daniel again to connect it all. Daniel Ryan. Sandy-blond hair, gorgeous smile, sparkling blue eyes. Perfectly pressed collar. *Georgetown graduate. Business and Political Science major. Manager of Operations at RogenCorp.*

He's attractive in a pretty-boy sort of way. I recognize him from Raven's last few parties. He's been spending more time with her lately, although I've never seen footage of what happens when they're alone.

I flip forward again and resume my study. The list of politicians backed by Titus is extensive. Whitcomb. Douglas. Bruno. The names and faces begin to blend so I exit the category to go through household information. I swipe through two maids and three cooks—Sofia, Pam, Charles, Joseph, Lorraine—before entering a section labeled "Security."

The bios are shorter here. No personal information. Name and job duty only. Gus is here. As well as the two men who escorted me to my new home. According to this, their names are Deitrich and Tamlin. I recognize another few from the video footage I've seen, men shadowing Raven as she shops. I keep swiping. Titus is either very prepared—or very paranoid. The list of his security team far outnumbers the list of staff and Raven's friends combined. I stop when I land on the last one and can't help but stare at his photo.

Linc Crawford is twenty-one at most. His dark brown hair is cropped close to his head and lays flat. He isn't celebrity handsome, as Ida would call it, but he is striking. He holds his jaw tight and fierceness shows through his brown eyes. He looks formidable. And like maybe he has a secret.

Someone knocks and I swipe a finger across the screen, removing the image of the boy. "Come in," I say, feeling silly that they would wait for my command when we all know it's locked from the outside.

At my invitation, the knob turns and the door swings open. A girl not much older than me pushes a cart into the room. Her lean body is the color of dark walnut, her arms slender but strong. The cart is made of metal and laden with an array of covered dishes and steaming containers on both the upper and lower racks.

"Good morning, Sofia," I say, recalling her name from the tablet.

"Morning," she says, busying herself with uncovering dishes and loading them onto a tray. I watch her pour coffee into a delicate, white mug and my mouth waters. We are never allowed coffee in Twig City. I sneak it from the Overseers at the quarterly mixers but it's always watery and bitter, as if it was made too light and left to sit too long.

Sofia hands me the mug. I take a sip—it is creamy and thick. "Perfect," I tell her.

I lean back to allow her to set the tray across my lap. She stands back, surveying the meal. "Anything else, Miss Rogen? Would you like me to lay out your clothes?"

"No, I can manage fine on my own." I inhale and soak up the scent of hot eggs and oatmeal. "Thank you so much."

Her head snaps up in surprise. "Uh, you're welcome," she says stiffly as she opens the door and pushes the tray out.

I shake my head, realizing the gratitude was an error. Raven doesn't do things like that. But as soon as I've taken my first bite, I don't care that I've slipped up. The food is delicious. Nothing about it is processed or rewarmed. The eggs are hot, the fruit fresh, and the coffee strong. There's even a tiny pot of honey to drizzle on the bread. I eat it slowly—for Lonnie.

I am propped on pillows, scrolling through the tablet, when Gus pokes his head into the room. He is already frowning.

"Get dressed. I'll be back in twenty minutes."

I scavenge the dresser and closet and discover the latter is large enough to stand inside. I can stretch my arms out to both sides and still not touch the clothes hanging on the racks, which almost makes me smile. I pass by silk gowns and chiffon skirts and gawk at the shelves of shoes.

Near the back, I find black tailored pants and a rose-colored blouse. Not exactly the bland jeans and T-shirts we all wear in Twig City. Then again, I don't expect Raven Rogen owns a pair of jeans, especially ones with holes in the knees. I used to fuss at Lonnie for purposely ripping her pants, but after a while, I caught myself doing it, too. In a sea of sameness, I needed to do something to feel different. I suspect that was Lonnie's reason also, although she would say she just liked the ventilation.

Turning to look at myself in the full-length mirror, I find that my blond locks have graduated from bed head to zoo animal. I do my best to smooth it, lacing it into a tight braid, and try not to think about the fact that I'm going to see Titus again. Creator. Father. Ugh.

I shudder.

Gus isn't waiting for me when I emerge from the bathroom. Instead, Deitrich, the driver from yesterday is there, standing half in, half out of the open doorway. "Ready?" he grunts.

"Ready," I say, although I have no idea for what.

I follow him into the foyer, expecting Gus or Titus or even Sofia, but that's not who waits for me inside. Instead it's *him*—the one from the photo. The security boy with a secret.

He's wearing a black jacket and his shoulders are broader in person. I peg him for a soldier, though he doesn't wear a uniform. His hands are tucked deep in his corduroy pockets and he is scowling at me. Despite the negative reception, my stomach somersaults.

He doesn't speak as his gaze sweeps the length of me and settles on my face. His expression is hard, as if looking at me is the last thing he wants to do.

"At least you're wearing pants," he says finally.

"Excuse me?" My voice gets stuck in my throat. Partly because he is a boy and I have almost zero experience conversing with males. And partly because he is so beautiful and Authentic that it makes my cheeks burn.

"Are you ready?" he asks, frowning.

I blink. "For what?"

"For our ride," he says, drawing out the words like I'm slow.

I think back to the Raven's schedule on the tablet. There wasn't time to memorize it, but . . . "What ride?" I ask.

Instead of suspicion, he regards me with impatience. "Didn't your father tell you? Or do you need me to write down your itinerary?" he snaps.

50

I glare at him, irritation flaring. In Twig City, I am used to condescension, but now that I'm Raven Rogen, I'm almost positive I should demand more respect. He continues before I can argue.

"Mr. Rogen wants me to take you out for a ride. He thinks it'll be good exposure for your . . . assailants." He picks up a leather jacket draped over the back of the couch and hands it to me. The colors match his, with the sleeves and cut trimmed for a female. "You'll want this. Helmets are downstairs."

"Helmets?" What could we possibly be doing that required helmets?

He gives me a withering look. "Come on."

I follow him out, swallowing back the rest of my questions. Voicing them will give away my ignorance or my fear. I can tell that Linc, for all his intriguing good looks, wouldn't welcome either. He clearly doesn't want anything to do with Raven.

I don the jacket as I walk, hurrying to keep Linc's pace. It zips into place, a snug fit against my thin blouse. Linc gives it a once-over and grunts.

Deitrich and another guard are waiting for us when we step into the lobby and follow us outside like unobtrusive shadows. The sun is still struggling to rise above the tops of the buildings that block it, leaving the morning air damp and earthy. Traffic is light here but farther down, at the intersection, I see taillights creeping along, one behind another.

While I tip my head up and inhale deeply, the men get into a black SUV parked at the curb.

"They're going to follow at a distance," Linc explains. "We're this way."

I have to force myself to follow when all I want is to dance and shout and absorb every particle of the outdoors. Linc leads us down the sidewalk toward a delivery truck. I don't see what's tucked behind it until we're standing in front of a motorcycle.

Chrome handlebars and a matte metal frame come together around a shiny black tank before it all slides into a cushioned seat. I don't comprehend a single thing about all of the gadgets and buttons, but they seem capable of more power than one vehicle should have. I falter in my step and stare at the metal monster Linc intends to operate.

His head tilts and a hint of a smile plays around his mouth. "Have you ever ridden one?"

I am tempted to say that I've barely ridden in cars, let alone a motorcycle, but I don't. "It's not enough that there are people trying to kill me, now they're going to let a machine have a go at it?"

Linc's grin widens and, despite my trepidation, my lips curve into a smile, too. But abruptly, as if catching himself, Linc's smile disappears, replaced by narrowed eyes and drawn brows. He steps up to the motorcycle and unstraps a helmet from the handlebars.

"Put this on," he says in a gruff voice, back to business. I set the hard shell on my head and fumble with the strap underneath my chin. With a huff, he pushes my hand away and takes over, nimbly working the snaps into place.

The helmet feels heavy and bulky around my ears when I move my head. My stomach jumps from anticipation and fear as I eye the motorcycle. There's something sensuous about it—like whispered danger.

"The main thing to know is how to turn. You have to lean

into it and let the bike do the rest. If you're not sure, press against me and move when I move. Got it?" Linc says.

I don't really, but I nod anyway.

"Just do what I do," he adds.

He helps me into a pair of gloves that are slightly too big, and then we're ready. He swings a leg over the seat and knocks the kickstand back in a practiced move.

I stand there, eyeing all of the parts, and trying to figure out the best way to get on behind him without falling over. He turns the key and the bike revs to life underneath him. The growl of it echoes inside my skin. Linc looks over, and though I can't see his expression behind his helmet, it feels impatient.

"Get on," he says, voice muffled. He holds his hand out and I take it tentatively, trying to figure out where to step and where to grab as I slide in behind him. He waits a beat while I orient myself and then the engine revs. I wrap my arms softly around his midsection, feeling overly forward.

"You're going to want to hang on tight," he says, as if reading my thoughts. I'm hyperaware of my arms pressing into his ribs. The inside of my helmet heats as my cheeks burn, and I'm glad he can't see my face.

I tighten my grip. "Are you sure this thing is safe?" I can't help but ask.

He shakes with laughter and we roll forward. "Are you sure you want to know?"

Behind us, the black SUV takes up position and follows along. What sort of protection can they offer me out here? If Raven's attackers show themselves, is there any way for two men in suits and sunglasses following a hundred yards behind to do a bit of good? If someone is intent on killing Raven—on killing *me*—it seems as though knocking me off a speeding motorcycle would be on the list of easier ways to get it done.

But then Linc bears down on the throttle and the thought is left behind on a rush of wind and adrenaline. For someone to kill me, they'd have to catch us first.

The bike has a life of its own underneath me, humming and vibrating. Linc punches the gas, and it's smooth and sleek—and fast. The pavement rushes by and the wind flaps the edges of my jacket, and I curl my shoulders forward so that my chest is pressed to Linc's back.

The speed is exhilarating. I have the urge to throw my hands out and let the wind roll over me in a moment of perfect ecstasy. Then we hit a bend in the road and I think better of letting go. I lean with him, matching my shoulder dip to his. The motorcycle tips effortlessly and then rights itself again as the road straightens. It's pure magic.

The speedometer tips eighty and I'm sure I would blow away if I let go. Death rushes by, six inches from my toes, nothing separating me from it except my grip on Linc's midsection. I tighten my arms and grin wider.

"You all right?" he calls out, decelerating just long enough for me to hear him over the wind.

"Go faster!" I call back.

"You like it?" he asks, surprise coloring his voice.

"I love it!"

The throttle slides forward once again and we pick up speed.

The turns are scariest, both because of the speeds with which we take them and the way we lean. Each time we come closer to parallel with the pavement, I squeeze Linc's ribs. I don't think he can hear my intake of breath or my cries of panic, but he pats my hand reassuringly. The curve straightens out and I know we're grinning together now.

Soon the road gives way to warehouses, then businesses, closed and boarded, sidewalks littered with trash and sleeping bodies. Linc executes a tight U-turn and pulls back on the throttle. I'm forced to hold on or get swept away.

In no time at all, we are back inside the glitzy borders of downtown.

Linc pulls to the curb in front of a towering upscale mall. "This is your stop."

I dismount and stand off to one side, surprised by my stiff muscles. "What are we doing here?" I ask over the idling of the engine, pulling off my helmet.

"You're having lunch with your dad and your . . . Daniel," he calls back.

My heart skips a beat at the familiar name. Daniel. The pretty boy from Raven's list of friends. The one she might be dating.

Foot traffic is light here, but those who pass give me curious looks.

"Is it . . . safe?" I ask when Linc cuts the engine and joins me on the sidewalk. I gaze at the cars creeping past, the dark buildings looming over me. If there's a threat, will I be able to see it?

Linc shrugs. "I guess we'll find out."

The sun beats down intensely, and I shed my jacket. Linc does the same, throwing his over his arm. A worn square of paper flutters out of the pocket and lands on the ground, flicking back and forth in the delicate breeze. I grab it and turn it over in my hands.

Linc snatches it away, but not before I catch sight of a face. It is a boy, striking in his similarity to Linc, though this face is rounder, older. "Who is that?" I ask as he tucks it away.

Linc is quiet for a long time. The black SUV pulls up to the curb behind us, finally caught up. The two men are still inside the cab, statues of patience.

"That's Adam," Linc says finally. "My brother."

His answer intrigues me. I have no idea what it would feel like to have a sibling. Sometimes I think Ida and Lonnie are like my sisters but I suspect it's not the same. "You look like him. Are you close?"

He hesitates and then his voice goes flat as he says, "He's dead."

I can't help but flinch. For humans, they say dying isn't the end, but death is so final for me, a soulless being. Though if Linc's broken expression is any indication, the possibility of life after death isn't much of a consolation. "I'm sorry. What happened to him?"

"There was an attack on his employer. He was outnumbered and they killed him."

"His employer?"

"Adam ran security for Senator Ryan and his son. They survived. Adam did not." He presses his lips together and goes silent.

I don't push. It's clear he doesn't want to discuss it further, and I can figure out most of the pieces for myself, thanks to Titus's tablet. Daniel Ryan is the senator's son; Adam died saving him. And then I realize: Adam's story sounds an awful lot like the situation Linc and I are currently living out.

I put my hand on his arm. "Linc, you don't—it's not worth it. *I'm* not worth it. Don't die for me."

He glares at me, his expression so cold I shrink back.

"Don't be ridiculous," he snaps. "None of this is for you. It's a job and I have my orders. Now come on. Your admirers await."

Linc's shoulders are an unapproachable wall of determination as he spins on his heel and leads the way inside. I follow without protest. His words have hit like a splash of cold water in the face. He's only doing his job. Now it's time I do mine.

CHAPTER EIGHT

THE MALL LOBBY buzzes with voices. To my left is a jewelry store with glass counters and muted lighting. A few customers silently browse through diamond necklaces and pearl earrings. To my right is a café with tables for two set up along the sidewalk beyond. At the far table, a young man leans in toward his date and takes her hand. He says something and she smiles softly and lowers her lashes. I stop short, soaking up their romance, their connection.

Someone steps up behind me, breaking my attention. I look back as Linc presses in near my left shoulder. His gaze lands on the couple and he frowns. I try to ignore the way his reaction deflates my enjoyment.

"We need to keep moving," he says quietly.

I tug my thoughts into line. I am Raven Rogen. I shop daily. I am unconcerned with things like romantic lunch dates and hot-headed motorcycle riders who hate me.

Linc and I join the other two guards and move as a group through the lobby. The elevator is open and waiting for us to file inside. One of the dynamic duo presses the button marked

Twenty. My stomach swooshes, but already I am getting used to the sensation.

A minute later, the doors shudder back open and deposit us on the twentieth floor. This lobby is darker, a hallway of muted earth tones leading toward a set of glass doors at the end. They are painted with curving letters that spell out "Fuego." Through the frosted glass, a tall counter separates me from a freckle-faced hostess.

She smiles when I enter and I do the same, though my version is colder. Full of polite condescension. It is an expression I've practiced a hundred times with Josephine, but feels strange now that I am using it for real. I am truly not myself in this moment. Which, I suppose, is a good thing.

"Miss Rogen." The girl greets me with a nod. "Your father is already seated with Mr. Ryan. Right this way."

The hostess leads us through the dim dining area dotted with sleek, round tables. It's not crowded, and the few patrons it holds are dressed in suits. I don't see Titus anywhere, but then the waitress takes us around a partition to a private room with a breathtaking view of the cityscape.

Titus sits at the head of a table with seating for six but only set for three, wearing a slim-cut charcoal suit. He's deep in conversation with the young man seated at his elbow. Daniel Ryan. He looks like a walking, talking version of his glamour shot from my tablet. Crisp collar. Gleaming teeth. Perfectly cut suit and expertly mussed hair. Something about the precision of it all makes me distrust him.

Behind them, with his back to the window, is Gus. Linc and my other two guards leave my side and join him there. Linc's posture is rigid, his hands clasped behind his back. He raises his chin when he catches me watching. I feel my cheeks burn and look away—straight at Titus. He has risen from his seat to greet me. He scrutinizes me with a hard-set jaw.

"Hello, Father," I say, hyperaware of all the eyes trained on me.

Finally, he nods. "Glad you could join us," he says before taking his seat again.

Daniel comes around the table and greets me with a quick kiss on the cheek. It is a normal enough greeting in Raven's world, but for me, the contact is jarring. For some reason, I think of Ida. She'd be ecstatic. I've just had my first kiss.

"Good afternoon," he says. Then he lowers his voice and adds, "Missed you, kitten."

"Good afternoon," I echo loudly enough for Titus to hear, ignoring the rest.

Titus sweeps his hand toward the seat on his right. "Come. Join us."

I move to the indicated chair but Daniel tugs on my hand. "Sit with me." He leads me to his side and holds out the chair next to his. Titus doesn't argue so I slide onto the cushion without objection. My nerves are pulled tight. I can feel Linc's disapproval, though I'm not sure for what.

Daniel eases in next to me, scooting his chair subtly left so his leg brushes mine underneath the cream-colored tablecloth. My heart thuds in my chest. Am I supposed to leave my leg there or pull it closer to my body?

A waitress appears with lemon water and salads topped with fresh green peppers and Roma tomatoes. I am three bites in when

I feel Daniel's eyes on me. I know that somehow, I've already done something wrong.

"Darling?" Daniel says questioningly, his brows raised.

Titus looks up sharply from his mobile device, and I follow his gaze to my plate. I mentally scan through my training videos, but come up blank. Does Raven never eat? I set my fork aside and sip my water in what I hope is a normal move.

"Daddy made me ride that terrifying excuse for road transportation this morning." I turn my voice into a stage whisper and add, "That security boy is mental. He drives like a maniac. I need something to settle my stomach."

I dare to make eye contact with Linc, who is watching our exchange intently, then look back to Daniel.

Daniel chuckles. "Sounds exciting to me. A mini-adventure. I was just telling your father he should give me some time off so that you and I can get away for real, maybe go on an adventure of our own."

"Soon, perhaps, but you know how busy it is around election time," Titus says, tiny lines appearing around the corner of his eyes. "So many functions to attend and ducks to put in a row, so to speak."

Daniel's fingertips brush my thigh as he smiles innocently at Titus. "Maybe around the holidays then, boss."

"Yes, maybe then," Titus agrees, as if I am not sitting here and able to answer for myself. In a very real sense, I suppose I am not able to answer for the girl named Raven Rogen.

Our meal resumes, and though I'm starving, I force myself to pick at the fresh veggies, moving them around more than I put them on my fork.

"Any word on the petition?" Daniel asks.

"It's moving forward nicely," Titus tells him.

"Terrific," Daniel says. "The poor are growing more and more volatile. You'd think having nothing would crush their spirit, not the opposite." Distaste coats his words.

"They'll tire eventually," Titus says. "Our main holdup is Senator Whitcomb's reservations about supporting the rezoning bill."

"He's against it?" Daniel asks.

"Just needs . . . convincing."

Daniel's brow quirks. "And if he isn't able to be convinced?"

Titus shrugs. "He knows the stakes."

Daniel grunts his approval. Titus glances my way and they both fall silent. A moment later, they begin speculating about the upcoming election and polls and various hot-button issues. I zone out, wishing I could eat the cream of mushroom soup the waitress has just brought, until I catch the words "economic segregation."

I remember the Authentics we passed on my way into town yesterday and look up. "You want to kick people out of the city because they don't have money?"

Both men turn to stare at me. Titus looks furious at my blunder, his brows pinched and his cheeks red. I fumble with my spoon, unsure what to do. I shouldn't have said that—or anything at all. But it's too late to take it back.

"Of course," Daniel says, clearly confused by my lack of support. "Their sense of entitlement has made them lazy and violent. They can't be allowed to taint what we've built here." Daniel's tone conveys his complete commitment to his words. "Don't you think?"

"She really doesn't think, Daniel." Titus laughs. It's harsh, unkind—chiding. "She's too caught up in her own little world of clothes and shoes."

Be her, his eyes demand.

Luckily, Daniel laughs lightly, as if this is a familiar idea where I'm concerned. "This girl and her wardrobe," he agrees.

"You're just jealous of my keen fashion sense," I tell him haughtily. Both men chuckle, and Titus relaxes his grip on his glass.

I stare down at my soup, suddenly hating the expensive waft of Daniel's cologne. I sneak a glance at Linc. He's staring stonily at Daniel but catches me watching and holds my gaze for a nanosecond. Something flashes deep in his eyes but it's too quick to identify.

When all of the plates have been cleared, Titus picks up his cell phone and returns his attention to the screen. He scans it with a deepening frown. "It's RogenCorp. I need to take this," he says, shoving to his feet.

"Anything I can help with?" Daniel asks.

He looks at Daniel, then me. "Later. You two can finish here first. Take your time. The guards will take you home when you're ready."

"Yes, sir." Daniel's hand settles on my thigh. My leg jerks reflexively, but if Daniel notices my sudden stiffness, he doesn't react.

After Titus leaves, taking Gus with him, Daniel turns in his chair. "Wait outside," he snaps at my entourage by the window.

Though the first two guards comply immediately with nothing more than a shrug, Linc hesitates, scowling. I send him a silent apology, knowing better than to contradict Daniel's wishes. I'm her now. I want what she wants, whatever that is.

Eventually, Linc disappears around the corner of the partition.

The moment we're alone, Daniel's hand on my thigh shoves upward an inch. Then he leans into me and presses his lips against the space just below my ear.

I sit primly on the edge of my high-backed chair, unyielding. I have no idea what Raven's response would be here. He seems too familiar with her body—my body—for this to be a first. His lips dip lower on my neck, leaving a trail of kisses down to my shoulder. He moves my blouse back, his fingertips brushing my bare shoulder. Before I can stop myself, I flinch.

He straightens and his hand falls away. "Are you all right?"

"I'm fine." I concentrate on breathing in and out slowly because this stupid boy is not worth blowing my cover. "Still just a little jittery from the attack the other night and—" I gesture around the half-cleared table, thinking fast "—this is hardly a romantic spot."

Daniel frowns and glances around. "Walk with me." He pushes to his feet and offers a hand. His grip is firm as he leads me a short walk away from our table to the empty space along the windows. The view pulls me in once again. I am struck by the miniature-looking rooftops and the Authentics moving like ants over the sidewalks far below us. I lean in, watching them scurry in their haste to spend more money, consume more food and drink. But the twenty-story hollow space between me and the street below brings on a sensation I'm unprepared for.

Dizziness washes over me and I lurch forward. Daniel pulls me upright. "Whoa."

"Sorry, the . . . height . . ."

That same perplexed expression returns. "Heights have never bothered you before. Are you okay?"

"I'm fine. It's just a long way down," I say weakly.

Daniel's lips tip upward. "Well, lucky for you, I'm here to catch you if you fall."

He says the words slowly, suggestively, as he leans in once again. I press my back against the window, at a loss. How could Raven Rogen possibly find him alluring?

Invisible insects crawl over my skin as he slides his arms around me and pulls me close. He is smiling down at me, his lips twisted in a way that belies any warmth behind the gesture. His breath, smelling of sour cream soup, hits my face. I deny the urge to shrink away for as long as I can, but when I can take it no longer, I pull away.

"Actually, I'm not feeling very well after all," I say. "I should probably get home."

But he just smiles slyly. "I love it when you make me work for it, Rav," he says. Before I can react, he grabs me and yanks me against him. His kiss is rough and hot, bruising my mouth with the force behind it. I struggle but it only makes him grab tighter, kiss harder.

When he comes up for air, his chest heaves and his eyes gleam with pleasure. His mouth is hovering over mine and I know he intends to go back for more.

I duck sideways, finally squirming from his grip.

"What's up with you today?" he says, his eyes narrowing.

Backing up awkwardly, I say, "I told you, I don't feel well. I want to go home."

"You don't feel well?" he repeats, as if he can't believe some-one wouldn't jump at the chance to make out with him. A shadow passes over his face and suddenly, his eyes blaze with anger. I shrink back. Clearly, this is a man used to getting what he wants.

"Sorry, I just—"

He grabs my arm, cutting me off. "Who do you think—?"

And then a voice sounds behind me. "The lady wants to go home," Linc says. "I think it's best if you step aside."

Daniel whips his head around, and loosens his grip on me. I scurry out of reach.

I watch as Linc faces Daniel with squared shoulders, hands light at his sides. He looks completely relaxed and utterly lethal.

"What did you say to me?" Daniel demands.

"I said you should step away. Now."

Daniel's shoulders stiffen. "Are you threatening me? Because that would be damn stupid of you."

"I'm simply reiterating Miss Rogen's request." Linc's tone is even, giving nothing away, but I see his fingers curl slightly inward.

Linc and Daniel regard each other. The air is heavy with ten-sion. Finally, Daniel blinks and mutters something under his breath that I can't hear as he grabs his jacket off the back of his chair and storms off.

I don't move until he has disappeared around the curve in the hall. Linc steps into my path, blocking me. I don't want to look at him. If I see pity in his expression, I think I'll lose it. My wall is close to crumbling, and I refuse to let him see that. To let Titus hear about it.

"Are you all right?" he asks.

Oddly, it is anger I hear in his voice, not concern. I raise my face to his.

"I'm fine," I manage. I've said this word more times in the last twenty-four hours than my entire existence.

"Are you sure? Because you've never—" He breaks off, his expression clouding.

"I've never what?"

He is silent and unwilling to look at me. Suddenly, I need to know what it is Authentic Raven has never done.

"Linc?"

"You've never turned down a boy," he says quietly.

My eyes fall quickly to the floor. "Oh." Suddenly, I'm ashamed for something I've never done.

The silence that follows is awkward and bloated.

I sidestep him and make for the exit, unsure which of us wants to escape the other more. Linc shadows behind me. I refuse to turn and let Linc see the effect of his words, but I have no choice when I reach the elevator. I step inside first. My two suited guards join us without a word or a second glance. Robots of intimidation. One of them pushes the button for the lobby and we coast downward in silence.

I don't meet Linc's eyes but I sense them locked on me, studying. Anger filters in. I hate that he can hurt me so easily—this boy with a broken past and a bad attitude. I hate that he makes me feel fragile. The anger makes it easier and I manage to glare at him until he looks away.

Outside, the men surge past me in an effort to scout out the surroundings. Linc stays out of reach but when I turn for the motorcycle, his hand lands on my arm. I shake it off.

"I think you've had enough excitement for one day," he says.

His patronizing tone heightens my embarrassment. "How do you expect me to get home?" I ask sharply.

"Deitrich will drive you." Linc gestures to the SUV still parked at the curb. One of the men waits patiently beside the passenger door. Like it's already been decided. Once again, I'm the last to know.

"Fine." I stride away from Linc, yank the door open, then close it was a satisfying slam. Using anger as a mask is a strange feeling. Using it, I feel more like Raven than myself. And then I realize. Her anger *is* her power. And now her power is mine.

CHAPTER NINE

TITUS AND I dine alone the next morning. He makes small talk, asking how I slept and if I like my eggs. He is taking his time with me today. A cat swatting playfully at the mouse before it moves in for the lethal blow. After our plates are cleared, Titus pours me a cup of steaming tea. I begin to lift the cup to my mouth but Titus stops me.

"You take your tea with sugar."

My hand falters as I set the cup down with a clink against the saucer. I fumble with the assortment of glassware until I pick out the sugar and load a spoonful into my cup. My movements are quick and jerky, giving away the anxiety coiling inside me.

"Daniel didn't stay very long after I left lunch yesterday." His voice is light as razor-tipped feathers.

"No, I guess he didn't," I say, using every ounce of training to keep my voice even. I sip my tea and pretend I'm unconcerned.

"Did he not find your company enjoyable?"

"You'd have to ask him."

Titus sets his tea down before meeting my eyes. His gaze is

direct, challenging, offensive. He knows I did something wrong. Something unRaven. Still, he doesn't call me on it, which scares me far more than if he had.

Behind him, Sofia moves unobtrusively along the paneled wall, assessing our needs. Identifying them before we do. Titus is a master of seeing and ignoring her all at once. He gives a subtle flick of his wrist and she retreats from the room.

"Did you have a chance to finish looking over the tablet?" he asks. His tone sharpens as he circles closer to his point.

"Yes, sir."

"And do you feel confident about your ability to identify those within your social circle?"

"I believe so."

The lightness vanishes. His eyes sharpen to a feral gleam. "You *believe so*?"

"I could use more time. I—"

His cup returns to the saucer with a sharp clatter. He leans forward, his next words made more dangerous by his proximity. "You should not need more time. You were bred for this, and so far, you're failing."

"I understand," I say quietly.

"Do you? Because if you did, yesterday would've gone much differently," he says. "Let me be clear about what is expected of you. Whatever Daniel suggests, you perform. Whatever Taylor admires, you purchase. Whatever *Raven* would do, you do it."

My stomach roils at what he's suggesting. Especially with Daniel. The memory of his lips on mine makes my skin burn. I let my hair fall over the side of my face to hide my blush.

"Yes, Father," I mumble.

His gaze sharpens. "Something else to work on is your attitude," he says. "My daughter is sure of herself and lowers her face to no one. Including me."

There is the unmistakable hint of challenge. I force my chin up and meet his stare. "Yes, *sir*," I say, packing as much acid into the last word as possible.

He nods, as if my answer—the vehemence in my tone—is exactly what he wanted to hear. "There is a party tonight, an opening of a new wing at a museum, and your performance will be flawless or there will be consequences." He tosses a linen napkin from his lap onto the table and stands up. "Gus will escort you to the gym."

He strides out with heavy footsteps.

Consequences.

The word trails in his wake, a tsunami of possibilities. Would he send me back? Given what Anna said on my last day, do I *want* to go back?

I sit rigid in my chair, staring at nothing while I concentrate on not hyperventilating.

That evening, Sofia thumbs through waves of fabric hanging in my closet while I watch. If she's surprised that Raven Rogen has asked for her fashion advice, she doesn't show it.

She stops on a purple halter-top gown. The skirt is layered with gauzy fabric that reminds me of tissue paper. "This one," she says, shoving it at me. "This is perfect for tonight."

"Are you sure?" I ask, eyeing the tiny swath of fabric.

She looks at me quizzically, and I remember I'm supposed to want to wear this sort of thing. "I'm sure. Mr. Titus will approve," she says.

"Of course. As do I." I force flippancy into my words. "I'll get changed."

She regards me for another moment, her mouth open as if to add something.

"Yes?" I ask coldly.

She shuts her mouth, opens it again. "Nothing."

I don't exhale until the door clicks shut behind her. For once, when the lock twists, I am relieved.

The dress is short in the front with a long, gauzy train in the back. The gym shorts I wore in Twig City covered more than the front of this dress does. I stare at myself in the full-length mirror and pretend this is exactly the sort of thing I want to be seen in until an impatient knock sounds at the door.

"Come in," I call.

The lock slides free and the door opens. Linc pokes his head in. His eyes widen as he takes in the sight of my dress and then immediately narrow.

"It's time to go," he says, swinging the door wider to allow me passage.

He is dressed in black slacks and a pressed white shirt. It is more formal than yesterday's ensemble of dark denim and cotton. I suppose he is trying to blend in tonight, but his plan is going to backfire. He looks deliciously dangerous.

"Raven," he says in a gravelly voice. I pause. I am standing so close I catch the scent of cologne. His breath is hot and minty against the tip of my nose.

"Yes?" I manage.

He clears his throat, eyes flashing in irritation. "You forgot your coat."

The way he slips from hot to cold rubs my emotions raw. I slide my arms into the jacket he offers, pretending I don't want to slide them along his chest instead.

Titus and Gus wait for us by the elevator. Gus is in his usual black-on-black security uniform. Titus is dressed in a dark suit that shines with newness. It makes his shoulders appear wider. I wonder if he's trying to look taller or if it's an unintentional side effect of the fabric's cut. He doesn't seem the type to need cosmetic reassurances.

My heels leave the soft carpet and make a sharp click against the heavy marble. Titus looks up and gives me a once-over that tightens my muscles. He gives a barely perceptible nod, and then presses the button for the elevator. I guess I pass his inspection.

Gus turns to Titus. "I assessed the threat level for the vicinity. The Contemporary Museum of Art has so many vulnerabilities—" he says in a low voice.

"That's exactly what we want," Titus cuts in. "The more vulnerabilities, the quicker they'll try again. Just have the men ready. I want them alive. I want names."

Gus's mouth tightens. "Yes, sir."

Panic bubbles in my chest. The men glance my way, and I pretend to adjust my shoe. The elevator bell dings and the doors slide open. I step inside and stare at my reflection in the door, wondering how my dress will look stained with blood.

CHAPTER TEN

THE ENTIRE CAR ride, Titus's mood is heavy. His cold distance is a reminder of what he expects when the car stops and the doors open. Gus and Linc sit across from us on the bench seats with a third guard I recognize but whose name I can't recall. I catch Linc watching me twice and both times I am the first to look away.

When we arrive at the Contemporary Museum of Art, I pile out between Titus and Gus and follow them to the main entrance. Streetlights illuminate every inch of pavement and glint off the shiny steel balcony that wraps the building several stories above our heads. Beyond the iron railing, neon lights in muted blues and greens spill out from gaping clear glass windows. The effect is modern to the point of cold.

There is a fair amount of hustle and bustle on the sidewalk, though this group is dressed more extravagantly than any I saw in the daylight. Tailored skirts have been replaced with sparkling gowns. Loose locks are piled high and hairsprayed enough to damage the ozone layer. Jewelry glints, heavy strands and pendants weighing women down as they make their way up the short flight of stairs.

When I reach the entrance, a man in a gray jacket holds the door open and nods as I pass through. "Miss Rogen," he says.

"Thank you," I murmur, trying hard to sound like I don't mean it.

Inside the lobby, artwork lines the walls; small, metal plaques label each piece. There is a sculpture in the center of the room, a woman made out of ribboned bronze with her mouth hanging open in a silent cry. For help or pleasure, I can't be sure. She has no eyes.

Titus and Gus walk ahead. Linc follows somewhere behind me and I am so focused on *being her* that I almost don't see a girl barreling toward me at full speed, her red hair waving around narrow cheeks as she bounds along.

"Hi!" she says happily.

I blink. Am I supposed to know her? She wasn't in my tablet . . .

Linc is at my elbow in an instant, tugging me back a step. The light pressure of his hand on my arm is infinitely comforting.

"Oh, sorry, I didn't mean to scare you," she says, her smile dimming to apologetic.

I struggle to seem calm and collected, determined to win the moment. Linc relaxes his grip. "Don't worry about it," I tell her.

"You're Raven Rogen, right?" Her attention shifts from me to Linc and back again. She pushes on without waiting for confirmation. "My cousin works here and I heard you might come tonight. I just love your outfit. Who's the designer?"

I look down at the girl's faded black dress, then try for haughty or impatient when I snap, "No one you could ever afford."

Before she can respond, I whirl away from her and head for the staircase that leads to the steel balconies and glowing lights. I focus on who I am supposed to be instead of the guilt that tugs at the base of my stomach—not who that girl thinks I am, or how Linc's hand on my arm makes me wish I could be myself. Shoving it all aside, I enter the party and smile widely, donning the mask.

The first thing I notice is the music. I can't see where it comes from but it is floaty and wistful in a way that makes my heart ache. Music in Twig City is rare, mostly children's songs and lullabies. Nothing like this.

I wander toward the sound, smiling and nodding at men and women in dark suits. No one approaches and I have the sense this is more Titus's crowd than mine. No one here is my age, and I don't see any of Raven's friends—not Taylor, not Lacey, not Brenna. Not even Daniel, though for that I am grateful.

After two laps around the room, I'm disappointed to realize that the music isn't live, just poured in through overhead speakers. But then I notice a hallway filled with more art. One piece in particular catches my attention and I pause to study it. Men in crisp black suits are painted onto an abstract, rainbow-colored background. They stand at formal attention with hands clasped in front of their bodies. Distinguished and purposeful except that their faces have been marked out in bright, bold red slashes. Faceless power. An apt representation of the world.

Farther down, female laughter bubbles, light and airy. Before I can turn to the next painting, someone grabs me from behind.

I spin quickly, terror and surprise mingling.

"What are you doing back here?" Linc demands.

"I was looking at the art," I say, looking down at his hand, which is still on my arm. I struggle to breathe normally.

He drops my elbow as if burned. "It's not safe to wander alone."

"I'm not alone. There are people everywhere."

"Exactly."

His condescension irritates me. I open my mouth to tell him so. Before I can form a response, the trilling laughter comes again from the exhibition room behind me, followed by my name.

"Raven! There you are!"

A petite blond appears in the doorway.

"Taylor," I say, oddly relieved to see her. The hours she and I have spent together via video make her feel strangely familiar to me. At least with her, I can know what to expect. Shallow, quick barbs, and a fake smile.

She inspects me critically and I hold my breath. "I didn't expect you out and about so soon after the attack. You look good, you know, considering."

"Thanks." My sarcasm isn't even feigned. Leave it to Taylor to backhand compliment her best friend after a near-death experience.

"I was thinking the same thing about you," I add, remembering how the assailant pushed her aside in the surveillance video. "But I should've known it wouldn't keep you away from a good party."

"Damn right." She glances over my shoulder, craning her neck to look around Linc. It's as if she doesn't even see him, but

I'm glad she ignores him. The only thing worse than Taylor's indifference is her interest.

She turns back to me without so much as a glance at him. "Did Daniel come with you?" she asks.

My response comes surprisingly easily. "It's not like he owns me," I say with a flip of my hair. "I'll call him tomorrow."

She smiles in an insinuating way. "Come on, let's make the rounds. These people need a dose of Taylor Douglas in their lives."

She loops her slender arm through mine and I let her lead me back toward the party and away from Linc.

We wander from group to group. Taylor does most of the talking, her tinkling laughter cutting through even the most serious conversations. She is a master at small talk and compliments, and leaves everyone smiling in our wake.

More than once, I feel eyes on me from across the room. I turn, expecting a glower from Titus or Gus's unsmiling watchfulness. Instead, I find Linc studying me with a careful, all-encompassing stare.

When we've done a full lap, Taylor leads me through a side door and into a dimly lit room containing rows and rows of coats. Small aisles span right and left, too narrow to walk through without my shoulders brushing the jackets hanging on either side.

"Shut the door, will you?" Taylor goes to the nearest rack and begins searching pockets.

I push the door until it latches and then wait while she continues patting down jackets. "What are you doing?"

"I had the party coordinator leave a present for us. Should be right around . . . here!" She pulls her hand free from the pocket of a fur wrap, grinning triumphantly as she clutches a clear glass bottle with blue lettering. Vodka.

She motions me over and pulls me down beside her. We sit on the carpet with our legs tucked under us. Taylor takes a quick swig, grins, and holds it out for me. I take it, trying to seem like I've done this a million times.

I wrap my lips around the opening and tip it back. The moment the liquid hits my mouth, it burns. I wrench the bottle away and squeeze my eyes shut to block out the fire ripping a trail down my insides. I swallow and then cough hard.

Taylor laughs. "Damn, Rav. Did the attack affect your ability to hold your liquor?"

As I grunt something that isn't really an answer, she grabs the bottle and takes another swig. All too soon it is my turn again. Like before, I cough and sputter as the liquid cuts a molten path down my esophagus. By the third swallow, the burning lessens and I feel . . . looser. Taylor is laughing, though neither one of us has said anything remotely funny. For some reason, this makes me laugh, too.

When the door opens, we fall abruptly silent, but that just makes the whole thing funnier and another giggle erupts from my closed lips.

I recognize Linc's shoes before I see his face. I manage to choke down my laugh, although I can't help the brilliant smile that remains. This relaxed version of me is elated to see him again and unconcerned with hiding it. He appears around the aisle of coats, glaring when he spots Taylor beside me—and the bottle between us. Only then do I realize neither of us bothered to try and hide it.

"Your father is looking for you," Linc says. His voice is low and his brows are drawn.

The image of Titus wipes the smile from my face in an instant.

I jump up, unsteady on my feet. "I'll see you later," I mumble to Taylor.

"Call me!" Taylor says as I hurry out. I can tell by the sound of her voice she has every intention of continuing the party on her own.

I follow Linc out the door and he whirls on me before I can leave the shadowy alcove that shields us from the rest of the party.

"Disappearing like that was monumentally stupid," he says.

"I didn't—I thought you were watching," I say, stumbling over words that feel thick in my mouth.

"You can't rely on me to be everywhere, to see everything."

"Why not?" I ask, cocking my head in genuine puzzlement. "Besides, it was just Taylor."

"How do you know? There could've been someone waiting for you in that room and I wouldn't have gotten there in time." He rubs a hand over his mouth and jaw. The hint of stubble grazes roughly against his palm.

I try to think of some flippant remark, some quick comeback to hide my fear or the fact that he is right, but my head is spinning and my thoughts are cloudy.

"And to top it off, you're drinking?" He throws up his hands. "Do you *want* to die?"

"No," I whisper, but he ignores me and keeps on.

"How am I supposed to protect you if you won't even protect yourself? I can't save an idiot. You're already dead if you keep this up."

I step back, feeling as if he's struck me.

Before I can answer, Gus walks up. He seems oblivious to the tension between Linc and me. "It's time to leave," Gus says.

"What happened?" Linc asks. His irritation with me instantly changes to a readiness for battle.

"There was an incident at the front door. Party crashers. They say it was a bunch of teenagers playing pranks but we're not taking chances. We're leaving now and taking the back way out." Gus looks at me. "Get your things."

I reach for the door to the coatroom but Linc shakes his head and steps around me. "Wait here." He disappears inside, but the sound of his voice lingers in my ears, an accusing loop of his harsh words.

Linc returns with my things and I follow him and Gus to the door. "Where's Titus?" I ask.

"He's busy," Gus says in a voice that doesn't allow for further questions.

In the lobby, he veers left. "This way," he says.

We double back down a narrow hall leading away from the main entrance and come to a halt in front of a service door. Linc holds my coat out. I shrug into it, eager to cover my exposed skin.

Gus pulls out his mobile device and scans the screen. "Come on, the car is waiting around back," he says to us before pushing through to the alley.

"Why do we have to go this way just because of stupid teenagers?" I ask. Partly because I'm her and partly because, after all the alcohol, I'm not myself.

Gus rounds on me with an incredulous expression, though Linc is the one who answers. His voice is laced with fury as he hisses, "Because you shot vodka in a coat closet at a museum opening in a dress that couldn't get shorter if you wore it as a shirt."

I cross my arms, defiant in the face of his temper. "Well, how is that any different than any other night?"

"Tonight, people may very well be trying to kill you," Linc almost roars back.

Without waiting for a reply, he shoves outside, his shoulders rigid. I want to snap back a retort but the liquor's made me slow. We walk a few steps in silence, Linc always half a stride ahead.

Around the corner, Linc's steps slow. "What now?" I ask.

"Shh." His arm darts out and pulls me up short next to him. Half a second later, he's shoving me sideways against the wall of the building. Linc and Gus exchange a look.

"What the—?"

"I said, shut up," he hisses. Something about his response, the lack of anger that was there a moment ago, catches my attention. I stare up at him with wide eyes. He scans the darkened space around us, his body creating a barrier between me and the alley. We're close. So close I could feel his breath if he turned toward me.

I want to ask him what the threat is but I don't dare make a sound. The silence is deafening. And then, farther out, something clatters to the ground.

"I'll be right back. Stay with her," Gus says.

Linc nods once and Gus disappears down the alley.

We wait.

Linc's chest rises and falls in a steady rhythm that belies a calm I can't muster. I breathe deeply, willing away the fog left by the vodka. Each minute that passes feels like a year.

Far off, feet shuffle. A thud sounds, followed by a beat of silence. And then, a scream, high-pitched but unmistakably belonging to a man.

Linc freezes. My hands clutch at the corners of my coat so hard I can't feel my fingertips. As if to prove we haven't imagined it, the scream comes again.

Linc's head whips around and our eyes lock. "Stay here."

That's the last thing I want to do, and once he's gone, the darkness presses around me. Shapes become dormant monsters. The quiet becomes a roar of violence. My feet itch to move, to escape. I'm too exposed here, pressed flat against the building with no cover. I take a tentative step toward a Dumpster. If I have to wait for Linc, it wouldn't hurt to do so from behind the cover of discarded debris. But Linc's words hold me back.

Another minute passes. Then another. I see the shadowed movement just before my assailant is upon me. I jerk sideways, but not in time to avoid a fist crashing into my stomach. I stumble backward and the momentum sends me hard against the wall of the museum. My back hits first, driving the air from my lungs, and then my head. My breath whooshes out of me in a grunt. The pain is instant and splitting, and cloudy splotches blur my vision. I swing out but connect with empty air.

The fist doesn't give me time to recover before it strikes again. I take a hit to the shoulder. Then another to my chest. My head lolls to the side. I try to fight back, to escape, but my knees buckle. I begin to crumple. A pair of arms dart forward and I flinch but it's not another punch. Instead, the hands slip underneath my arms to yank me up.

"Raven Rogen," a voice says. It's female, which startles me

enough for my eyes to open. I struggle to focus on the image swimming in front of me. A burning halo of orange hair frames a strikingly familiar face.

"I know you," I mumble. It's the girl from the lobby.

"You don't know anything," she says.

There is a moment of silence between us as she lifts her arm over me, a syringe clutched in her hand.

"No!" I jerk and struggle against her one-handed hold. She releases me long enough to land a stinging slap that drives my face sideways.

"Stop being so damn difficult," she mutters.

Where are you, Linc?

But before I can scream, her hand slides around my throat and begins to squeeze. I manage two very short breaths before my oxygen is cut off. I thrash wildly, kicking and clawing for purchase. Anything that will make her let go. But it's not enough. There is a sharp prick against the tender skin near the base of my neck. The needle presses against and then inside my skin. The contents of the syringe empty a strange coldness into my body, and a triumphant smile lights the girl's face.

"Gotcha."

"Raven!" Linc's voice sounds from down the alley

The girl swears under her breath, and her grip loosens. I try to yell for Linc to escape, but there's nothing left in my muscles to carry out the order.

The redhead leans into me and hisses, "This isn't over, product. I know your secret."

By the time I understand her words, she is gone and someone is kneeling over me.

"Raven, are you okay?"

Linc's voice calls me back for a moment. But then darkness edges into my peripheral vision and widens until it's all I see. Fog encroaches. My knees buckle. My lids droop. Then everything goes black.

CHAPTER ELEVEN

I WAKE, SORE and exhausted, in Raven's bedroom. The mattress feels like rocks underneath me. Sunlight streams through the curtains. I shift from my side to my back to escape the glaring light and wince at the pressure this puts on my tender shoulder.

I blink, each meeting of my eyelids sending shooting pain through my skull. Fabric rustles as someone leans in and tucks the blanket tighter around my shoulders. A familiar pair of brown eyes blurs into focus, a forehead creased with worry.

"Josephine? What are you . . . ?" I let the question trail off. The pounding in my head intensifies with each word.

"Hello, Ven." She smiles, her usually relaxed features pinched with forced cheer. Her tidy bun has come loose and several strands fall in disarray around her face. She's wearing tailored pants and a simple gold watch. It's the first time I've ever seen her in anything outside of scrubs or a lab coat.

My surprise must be evident because Josephine hurries to explain. "I came here to examine you after you collapsed. Titus wanted a doctor that understood your . . . differences, so I'll be staying here for a while to monitor you."

Collapsed. The simplicity of the explanation pricks me. How easily they dismiss violence in this world. How easily they dismiss me.

Josephine sinks onto the bed beside me, drawing open a black bag and searching its contents. "What happened? Do you remember?"

I squint into the memory. "There was a commotion. Gus went to investigate . . . and Linc. And then the girl came."

"A girl did this?" Josephine asks. The disbelief is clear. It might've been funny, the idea of one girl single-handedly defeating two trained guards and myself, but then the face of my attacker appears in my mind—the memory of that burning halo of hair.

The redhead's words replay in my mind. *I know your secret.*

I swallow a sob. Everything has changed. They want me. The attackers want *me*. Not Authentic Raven, but Imitation Ven. How is that even possible? Were they after me from the start? Or are these different assailants altogether, ones who discovered that the real Raven had been switched?

I struggle to sit forward, but Josephine's hands gently push me back. "Don't try to move just yet, darling."

She pulls a stethoscope from her bag and presses the cold metal to my skin. I flinch. Even the light contact of the metal reignites the sharp pain.

"It's all right," she murmurs over and over, comforting. She pulls out a small light and shines it directly into my pupils before asking me to recite mundane facts.

"Name?"

"Raven Celeste Rogen."

"Date of birth?"

"July twenty-second." I have to do the math on the year because while Raven is eighteen, technically, I'm only five.

"Address?"

"Eighteen-hundred H Street. Washington, DC."

"Today's date?"

"October nineteenth."

Josephine presses her lips together and dips her chin in a single nod. I sit back. My throat burns, my chest aches, and my back throbs. I remain carefully still while Josephine completes her examination.

"Believe it or not, I don't think anything's broken," she says. "The bruising to your jaw and neck is another story. And your chest and shoulder are going be sore."

"My head hurts," I whisper.

Josephine nods. "This should help." She hands me two white pills and a glass of water. I take the offered drugs, eager to end the pain.

"Thanks," I tell her when I've emptied the cup.

Josephine's pocket beeps. She wanders away as she pulls out a phone. In a few moments, the pills begin to work and the pounding lessens. By the time Josephine returns to my bedside, I'm lucid enough to want answers.

"How long have I been out?" I ask.

"Fourteen hours."

I lean forward, my eyes wide. "Is that normal?"

"Well, you were injected with a tranquilizer." An

indecipherable look crosses her face. "But it was longer than we anticipated. Then again, this sort of chemical has never been used on Imitations, so we had no data to base it on."

"Is it—am I going to be okay?"

"Yes. You're going to be fine," she assures me.

My eyes well with tears despite her reassurances. "It's not like I thought it'd be," I whisper.

It is the first and only show of hesitation in my role, but instead of scolding me, Josephine's expression clouds, a mix of guilt and pity. "Ven, I'm . . . you're doing an amazing job."

I touch her hand. It's not her fault I'm disposable. She's in the same boat as I am, taking orders and trying not to screw them up. The only difference is that she spends most of her days in the relative safety of Twig City.

"How are they?" I ask softly. "Lonnie and Ida?"

My chest aches even more when I think of them. I wonder if Lonnie is comforting Ida or if she's taken her usual "stiff upper lip" stance and expects Ida to do the same. Fragile Ida. She is not cut out for this, despite what they tell us about our chemical makeup and our being created to serve. I am glad that it is me and not her who has been called up.

Josephine lays a hand over mine. "They're well, Ven. They miss you."

I nod, fighting a sudden well of tears.

"Will you give them a letter for me?"

She hesitates only a second before she answers. "Of course."

I scrawl the picture message quickly, using a scrap of paper Josephine finds in Raven's nightstand. I write in our shorthand code and don't bother signing it: *The world is dangerous. Stick together. Miss you both.* Josephine watches but doesn't comment or ask about the symbols.

"There's something else. Titus wants you to get out more. Alone." She doesn't look at me as she says this, but I understand what she means. Titus wants me to dangle myself like a worm, see who takes the bait.

"How long do I have before that happens?"

She glances at my bruises. "A day. Maybe two. I don't think he'll wait longer."

I nod. It's not a matter of "if," only "when." Even Josephine knows that.

Josephine sighs. "I have to go but someone will check on you regularly. You should get some rest."

"Josephine," I call. She pauses at the door. "Thank you."

Her expression softens. "Good luck," she says before she leaves.

Alone once more, I slip back to sleep. My dreams are cloudy and nonsensical. In one scene, I'm back in Twig City, safe and sound with Ida and Lonnie. I'm happy in my own naiveté. In another, every Authentic I know is pointing a loaded gun at my chest, including Raven Rogen herself. I scream curses at them but they don't even blink.

They fire and my blood runs down my chest and arms into my cupped palms. I use it to slide free of the bars that suddenly spring up around me and then I am sprinting toward the edge, knowing there's no one there to catch me when I jump.

I wake late that afternoon to find a tray of cold soup and dried-out toast next to my bed. Butter has made the bread mushy in the center and stale at the edges. I put it back after only one bite and pick up a glass of orange juice.

"You should eat. It will help you keep up your strength."

The voice startles me, and I almost drop my cup.

Linc rises from his place in the corner and moves closer.

"You scared me!" My fingers tremble from the sudden surge of adrenaline.

"Sorry." The light from the windows illuminates the dark circles ringing his eyes. His hands are stuffed into his pockets and his mouth is pinched. "You were sleeping when I came in earlier. I didn't want to wake you."

"Why are you here?" I can't help but ask.

Linc sighs. "Your father wants to talk to you. You're to get dressed and meet him in the living room."

A ribbon of panic laces its way through my gut. "Talk about what?"

"How you're feeling. The attack." Lines appear as the edges of his eyes tighten. "And what comes next."

He's silent for a long time. There's something uncomfortably different about the way he's looking at me today. It's nothing obvious but it's there. In the way he doesn't glare every time he catches sight of my face. And in the uncertainty in his stance, like he can't decide whether to come closer or back away.

"Is he angry?" I ask finally.

"At you? No. But I let her get away." Linc's brows knit. There's more to his admittance than just Titus's disapproval. He's mad at himself. It makes me want to comfort him, which is silly. Linc is an invulnerable wall of toughness.

Even so, I shake my head and assure him. "If you didn't get her, no one could."

He smirks. "How do you know? You were knocked out."

"Linc, why do you do this job?" I ask. "There have to be plenty of safer options out there."

He shoves his hands into his pockets and stares me down but his gaze is far away. He is quiet for a long time before he says, "I'm not interested in being safe. And I'm not afraid to die."

"Then I'm all wrong for this assignment." The words are out before I can stop them. My breath catches in my throat.

"What are you talking about?"

The expression he wore that first day is back. Now I understand it: distrust.

"The death threats, of course. Being bait. It scares me," I cover. "I'm meant to be shopping, gossiping. Not this. I'm all wrong for this." I flip my hair for good measure and then wince.

"Huh," he grunts. "Well, you need to get better at it because they're not going to stop coming until they get what they want."

I shrug, ignoring the pain caused by lifting my shoulder. "I know you'll always save me." By the time I realize how naïve and pathetic my words sound, it's too late to take them back.

A shadow crosses over his face. "Not always."

"Until the threat's gone," I amend but it's belated and sounds lame even to me.

His eyes burn with something that is not quite anger but close. "This is not a world where you can afford to rely on someone else. You have to save yourself."

His words are a harsh dose of reality. Scared or not, he is

absolutely right. The danger is real and it's not fair to expect someone else to fight my battles for me.

These attacks aren't going to stop. And unlike Linc, death isn't a thought I can shrug off. When I'm gone, will it ever matter that I was here? Will anyone other than Lonnie or Ida even remember me or mourn my absence? Meanwhile, Linc is risking a life he doesn't appreciate for a girl who doesn't matter.

"Linc, you can't—don't—" *Die for me* is what I want to say. But last time I said that, it caused a fight. "Don't let him push you around," I finish instead.

In that moment, I make my decision. I'm not going to sit around and wait for someone to kill me. I can—and will—free myself. I have no idea how or whether it's ever been done. But I will escape. Or I will die trying.

CHAPTER TWELVE

AFTER LINC LEAVES, I head to Raven's closet. Getting dressed is painful. I pull on a sports bra and stand before the mirror in mild disgust. My white-blond hair is matted against my head, my lips are chapped, and there are dark circles underneath my eyes. Aside from the purple-and-blue bruises blooming around my neck and chest, I am even paler than I was while living underground.

I wonder if my appearance will make Titus take more pity on me . . . or less.

I find him in the living room, and I can tell by the set of his shoulders as he gazes out the window that he is cross.

"Father?"

He whirls around, with drawn eyebrows and fisted hands. I shrink back and clutch my hands together.

"Tell me what happened last night?" Titus barks.

I stand up straighter and gather my thoughts. "We left the party through the back—"

"Why?"

"I don't know. Gus led the way."

He frowns, but lets it pass. "Then what?"

"There was a noise and Gus went to have a look. We heard him yell and Linc went to check it out."

"He left you alone."

"Yes." Confirming it makes me feel like some sort of tattletale but I can't lie. Not about this. Not if my plan is going to work. *I must save myself. No one else will.*

"What happened once you were alone?"

"I tried to find a place to hide but the girl, the redhead, found me too quickly."

"She had red hair?" he interrupts. "You're sure?"

"Yes," I say, my voice scratchy. "I've seen her before. She talked to me in the lobby, asked me about my dress."

He frowns. "You're sure it was the same girl?"

"Positive." I know I have to tell him. Partly because I'm not sure what he'll do if he finds out I held back. But another part of me can't stand the uncertainty in my discovery. "There's something else. She knows what I am."

Titus blinks. "What do you mean?"

I relay her whispered words. "She called me a *product.*"

His jaw juts forward. "How is that possible?" he demands.

I don't have an answer but he doesn't seem to be speaking to me. He looks past me, at the gauzy curtains hanging on the window. I can see his wheels turning and despite what that girl did to me, I can't help but feel afraid for her.

"Have you told anyone else about this?"

"No, of course not," I assure him.

"Good. See that you don't." He strides to the living room's

side door, to a place marked Off-Limits on my house map. I wonder, not for the first time, what's on the other side.

"What does this mean?" I blurt out. "If they're after me for . . . me, instead of her?"

He pauses, his hand on the knob. Without turning around, he says, "It means nothing. Your purpose is the same. Do your job, draw them out."

The *or else* is implied.

When he leaves, the door slamming behind him, I sink back onto the couch, suddenly exhausted. I close my eyes, count to three, then exhale.

When I open them again, I notice a small, ivory horse on the mantel above the fireplace across from me. It stands on its hind legs, riderless and colorless except for the bright red of its tiny pupil. The angle of the animal exposes the eyes to two very separate views. One points toward the side door Titus left through. The other is aimed directly at where I sit on the couch and the exit behind me.

Curious, I stand and wander toward it. Halfway there, I realize the ruby red glints off the lamplight in a way that can't possibly be paint. I stop and stare, a bubble of dread rising and sticking somewhere halfway to my throat.

It's a camera.

And if I know Titus, it's only one of many. Each piece of art, each prominently displayed antique, could simply be an expensive decoy. Titus is watching everything, everywhere. But now, so am I.

Game on.

The next afternoon, I run laps on the roof. Each footfall sends a jolt of sharp pain through my bruised body, but I do it without complaint. Every moment I'm out of my room, moving around the grounds, is another moment to watch, to listen. To study.

I've spotted two other cameras besides the horse in the parlor. One was mounted inside a telescope in the library and another was wedged into an abstract painting that hangs across from the elevator at the front entrance. Both are so small, they're almost impossible to spot.

Even now, there are two along the edge of the roof near the track where I run. One points toward the door leading inside and one watches the uppermost landing that houses the tennis court and, farther out, a helipad.

When I'm not looking for cameras, I study the guards: their communication devices, their schedules, which exits and entrances they use, and how they move around the house. This morning Deitrich came in via the service entrance at the back. It seems his job is to man the hallways—grunting as he moseys his way along his route—and drive the SUV. Gus was already here when I woke up. Now that I think about it, it seems that Gus never leaves the house unless Titus does. His role seems to be standing near the door of whichever room Titus occupies, watching, a stiff sentry. Maybe he lives here. I've learned there are staff quarters off the dining room.

Linc hasn't arrived yet. His job is the worst of all, for me and for him: show up and leap in front of the bullet or fist while lecturing me in the process. Yet, when he's gone, he's the shadow I miss the most.

As I run, a single guard watches from inside the doorway. I

enjoy the solitude of being the only one outside. When I'm not so closely monitored, I feel a sort of lightness. The expectations and role-playing fall away and it's just me and my determination to find a way out.

Several laps in, the guard disappears and Linc saunters out. He leans casually against the wall, a bottle of water dangling from one hand. Even with dark shades covering his eyes, I feel the weight of his stare as my feet pound their way around the track. The ends of my hair tickle my shoulder blades as I run past him. I am hyperaware of the exposed skin between my cropped sports bra and the waistline of my shorts but I tell myself this isn't me— it's *her*, Authentic Raven, and he's seen it before. Or thinks he has.

I slow to a jog and then walk the last few steps over to him.

"Thanks," I say, taking the water.

Now that my feet have stopped moving, the bruise along my jaw throbs in time to my heartbeat. I hold the cold liquid to my face for a long moment.

"How are you feeling?" Linc asks.

"Like I got my ass kicked."

He snorts.

I take a swig of the water. When I lower the water bottle, I find Linc watching me. Or, more specifically, watching the bruises on my face. Very slowly, he raises his hand as if to reach out and touch the purpling mass marring my cheek.

I go still. My breath catches as I wait for his fingertips to reach me. Halfway there, he stops and blinks. His hand lowers again and shoves it into his pocket. I step back, out of the force field that is Linc, and try to pretend I don't care that he can't bring himself to touch me.

I resume walking, partly to let my body cool down and partly to escape the awkwardness of the moment. Linc falls into step beside me. The wind gusts are strong this close to the roof's edge and when he speaks, I have to strain to hear him.

"You missed the one pointing at the staff entrance."

"What?"

"There's a camera mounted inside the buffet on the east wall of the dining room. It points directly at the door leading to the staff's quarters. You failed to notice it yesterday."

I stare at him a beat too long, trying to read his blank expression. "I'm sure I don't know what you mean."

He lifts his sunglasses and rests them on his head, his gaze intense. "I saw you, Raven. Last night. After dinner. You tried to pick the lock to the entrance with a bobby pin."

"Must've been someone else you saw. I was in my room last night." I raise my chin in defiance against his accusations.

"I wouldn't mistake you for anyone," he says in a way that makes me shiver.

I don't tell him he already has.

"Look, I don't know what you're playing at, but whatever it is, you won't win. You're lucky I'm the one who saw the footage of you poking around there and not Gus or one of the others."

He's right, and we both know it.

"Why do you care anyway?" he goes on. "You've never been interested in that part of the house before."

What can I say that won't raise his suspicions even further? I put one foot in front of the other and stare at the roof ledge beyond the track. I can feel Linc's eyes on me, searching. I hope, for both our sakes, he comes up empty.

"My diamond bracelet is missing," I say finally, packing haughty indignation into the words. "Sofia was the last one in my room. I wanted to see if she took it."

I gulp more water to hide my flush of shame.

"You think Sofia stole from you?" Linc's brow slants as if he doesn't quite buy it but he's willing to humor me.

"I don't know. Who else could it be? You're the only other person who's been in my bedroom. And you don't exactly seem like the jewelry type."

Linc's lips twitch. "No, I'm more of a flowers-and-chocolate kind of guy."

For the first time since we began walking, I meet his gaze. We share a small smile. I can see the wall of distrust he's constructed between us but in this moment, it seems much more negotiable than it did before. I know exactly what sort of concession I'd have to make to break it down: the Truth.

And right now, that's the one thing I can't afford.

CHAPTER THIRTEEN

TAYLOR COMES FOR lunch on Tuesday, practically accosting me as I enter the dining room. Her brows are raised with practiced concern and morbid curiosity. The fading bruise on my cheek doesn't help matters.

"Are you all right?" Taylor asks, managing to hug me while barely touching me. "I heard about your close call the other night. I cannot believe the skuzzies out there who get their rocks off trying to hurt women. I mean, you could have been killed—or worse." She stops, newly horrified as she realizes what her words imply. "I mean, they didn't actually . . . touch you, did they?"

"No, they didn't," I say, wondering what her reaction would be if I could tell her my assailant was a woman.

"I bet Daniel was livid when he found out. Just beside himself with worry." She stops, cocks her head at me. "You did call him, right?"

"Who?"

"Daniel. Are you even listening to me?"

"I . . ."

She presses on. "Even though you guys aren't officially an item to the rest of the world, he would still want to know. I mean, three public appearances . . . that's practically engaged, which isn't a big deal since that's the five-year plan. But at least tell him so he can stay ahead of the press. A future RogenCorp president should be aware of anything going on with his potential fiancé."

Daniel being groomed to take over Rogen Corp makes sense; he's already the director of operations. But Raven Rogen, his future fiancé? That one catches me off guard. "You're right, I should call him," I say when I recover.

"Speaking of which, what's up with your cell? I call and call and it goes straight to voice mail."

I falter, unsure what to say. I hadn't thought of it until now, but whatever phone Raven Rogen owned has not been given to me. I wonder who Titus thinks I would call if he gave me one. "My phone is . . . broken. I dropped it when I was attacked."

"Ugh," she says, as if that is the most annoying part of what happened to me.

"I'll get a new one soon," I say, trying to emulate her annoyance. "My staff is useless."

She nods once, and just like that, moves on. For the rest of the meal, she does not speak of my attack again, not even when I reach across the table for the salt shaker, revealing the purpling bruise on the inside of my forearm.

I'm drifting along, half listening, when my foot knocks Taylor's purse over. A thick envelope slides out along with two tubes of lip gloss. I bend to retrieve the items and try to ignore

Taylor's irritated mutterings about being "more careful, geez."

"Sorry," I tell her, handing her the envelope. She snatches it from me and drops it back inside her righted bag. "What is all that?" I ask.

"Daddy made me stop and pick up a donator's contributions on the way here. I have no idea why the man deals in cash. It's not even traceable as a tax write-off." She shrugs. "But who am I to tell a billionaire how to do the books?"

Cash.

Untraceable cash. I've been so bent on how to get out of here, I haven't considered what I'd do once I'm free. I'll need money to survive and credit cards are out of the question.

When we're nearly finished eating, Sofia appears in the doorway.

"What?" I snap out, cringing inside as I do.

"Visitors," Sofia says, dipping her chin and casting her eyes downward.

"Who is it?" I ask, my stomach pitching at the thought of Daniel showing up unannounced.

But then two girls appear behind Sofia. I recognize them, but it's not a welcome surprise to have them here now. Lacey and Brenna, the West End Witches. I paste a smile on and do my best to hide my annoyance.

"Oh, good! You came," Taylor says, pushing to her feet. She goes to each girl and air-kisses their cheeks. I follow her lead.

"We wouldn't miss it. Hello, Raven," Brenna says as she gives me her cheek in greeting. Her brown hair is piled high on her head and bounces when she moves. The freckles dotting her nose give the illusion of a tan.

"I didn't know you were coming," I say to Lacey, bending to reach the petite girl's bony cheek.

"I forgot to mention I invited them," Taylor says by way of apology. "So glad you both could make it. Seems like it's been forever since we all caught up."

"Of course. We've been worried sick over Raven and these attacks," Brenna says. Her words are dripping with false concern, a tone I recognize easily from Raven's past interactions with these girls. She pats my arm with a manicured hand and I gesture toward the table to cover my distaste for her.

We all take a seat around the table. I wait while each of the girls plants a purse the size of a suitcase on the floor beside them. "Sofia," I call out. She appears at the doorway instantly. "Tea, please."

Lacey's phone rings and Brenna rolls her eyes. "Is that the same lobbyist who kept calling you through dinner last night?" Brenna asks.

Lacey's cheeks redden. "Maybe." She silences the call and stuffs her phone back into her purse.

"He's a total loser," Brenna tells us. "But Lacey's decided he's sweet because he spent last weekend visiting his mother."

"Maybe he's just a nice guy," Lacey shoots back.

Taylor and Brenna share a wry smile. "Oxymoron," Brenna says with a dismissive wave.

"Maybe he's gay," Taylor offers. "Using you to get to that hottie brother of yours."

Lacey's nostrils flare. Taylor's hit a nerve, as she no doubt intended. "Well, you should've seen Marco last night at the Cigar Room. Definitely not gay. Or nice."

Brenna laughs and then her brows knit. "Wait, Marco Jenner? I thought he was with Cami."

Taylor's eyes sparkle cruelly. "He is."

She and Brenna laugh again. I join in but it's more teeth than noise. These girls are vultures. I catch Lacey watching me, as if waiting for my opinion, so I say the first thing that pops into my mind. "You should call the lobbyist back."

Lacey's eyes widen in surprise. "You think?"

Brenna and Taylor stop laughing and stare at me. "Yeah, you think?" Brenna echoes, the undertone of her words issuing a challenge.

I ignore it and make sure I sound unconcerned. "If you like him, then call him. Don't let these two stop you. What do they know about men anyway? They're both single."

Lacey glances at the other two girls, whose mouths have fallen open. "All right. I'm calling him right now." She grabs her phone and disappears into the hall.

Brenna and Taylor glare at me. "What the hell, Rav," Taylor says.

"Yeah, that was rude."

I smile because it's ironic how often they've been so much worse and gotten away with it under the guise of a plastic smile. "I was just messing with you. Lighten up."

But the heated glares remain.

"Someone needs a little mimosa in her orange juice," Brenna mutters.

I wonder if it's worth pointing out how redundant that sounds. But then Taylor scrapes back in her chair. "I'm going to use the powder room," she says haughtily.

"I'll go with you," Brenna offers, pushing to her feet. She

casts a glance at me. "Maybe we can use the time to figure out men."

Taylor giggles. Brenna smiles. They've forgiven me. At least on the surface. I know what—or rather *who*—they'll discuss in the bathroom. I watch them go, waiting with a tap of my toe until they round the corner. As soon as I'm alone, I knock my napkin onto the floor. I'm careful not to glance in the direction of the camera Linc told me about—the one hidden underneath the lip of the buffet cabinet across the room. With my eyes on the floor, I slide out of my chair and crouch in front of Taylor's bag.

It's hanging open, an opportunity waiting. My fingers move fast as I lean down and reach inside, withdrawing a wad of bills from the envelope. I cover the contraband with my napkin and slide back into my seat, pocketing the bills as I move.

When I'm seated again, I frown down at the obvious bulge it creates in my fitted slacks.

Voices sound outside the doorway; I don't have more than a few seconds before someone returns. I cast about for a safe place to hide the money. With my napkin as a shield, I stuff it into the only place I can think of that will remain completely concealed until I'm alone. My bra.

I straighten in my chair and raise my glass to my lips just as Lacey returns, Brenna and Taylor trailing behind her. There is no more talk of the sweet lobbyist or Brenna and Taylor's offense at my teasing. Instead, they've already moved on to an upcoming party being thrown for a newlywed politician and his bride.

"He's more than twice her age," Brenna says with disgust.

"Yeah, but he's rich. He has that yacht and that vacation house in the Maldives. And you gotta admit, he's not bad for an old guy," Lacey says.

"You're both so shallow," Taylor says with a roll of her eyes. "He's poised for Senate. His platform is solid and he's got more than enough financial backing. He's a shoo-in and from there, who knows. The White House. If she hadn't married him, I might."

"Ew," Brenna says, wrinkling her nose. "You'd marry someone like that?"

"I'd marry a president," Taylor quips.

"I thought you wanted to *be* a president," Brenna says.

"If you can't be one, marry one," Lacey jokes.

The money is heavy and warm against my skin as the conversation swirls around me. I have no idea how much it is or how far it will take me. I've seen enough to know it won't last forever, but it's a start. Anywhere is better than seated here with these young women who act like middle-aged trophy wives.

"You're lucky, Raven," Taylor says, breaking into my thoughts. "Your dad doesn't expect any more from you than social support."

"You make me sound like a secretary," I tell her.

"No, it's a good thing. Sometimes I wish Daddy didn't expect me to be the first female president. Then again, I've worked so hard already, I have to believe it'll happen someday."

"It will," Brenna tells her. "You're ruthless. I mean that in the best way possible."

Taylor laughs. "Thanks."

I cringe inwardly as Taylor's phone beeps with a text. She reads it with a deepening frown. "I better get back," she says, picking up her purse and rising.

I do the same, trying to rein in my relief at being free of these girls.

Brenna and Lacey push to their feet and gather their purses. "We'll see you both on Friday?" Brenna asks at the door.

"Of course," Taylor says.

"What's on Friday?" I ask.

Taylor's eyes narrow. "Houten's. The fundraiser for Senator Whitcomb's campaign, remember?"

Brenna sighs. "I wish we didn't have to go, but Daddy says it's important to show support for Whitcomb since he's being reelected."

I do the math and even though I know I'm making some sort of blunder, I can't stop myself from saying: "But the election isn't for two more weeks. How do you know he'll be reelected?"

Brenna and Lacey wear matching expressions of confusion. Taylor skips straight to staring at me like I'm crazy. Her brows lift and her cheekbones follow. "Because we always know, silly."

I force a smile and shake my head a little. "Right. Duh. Sorry."

They look unconvinced but don't pursue it. Brenna and Lacey leave first, with Taylor not far behind. I watch them go, tracking their exit onto the street from the front window.

Houten's. I've seen it a few times in the video footage. It's an older brick building located downtown, always crowded and full of exits and alcoves.

My pulse accelerates at the thought of slipping out one of the many doors there, into the cover of night. Fading into the sea of faces and party dresses. Never to be recognized again. It is a bold move, attempting an escape right under their noses. But it's a promising one. And right now, it's all I've got.

CHAPTER FOURTEEN

BY THURSDAY AFTERNOON, I have examined every book, essay, and newspaper I can find in Rogen Tower. None of them mention what I'm looking for: Twig City. I wonder how many others from this world know its name or that it even exists. I'd wish I'd paid more attention when Marla had ushered me from the exit. If I'm going to run, I want to run in the opposite direction of Twig City.

A familiar stab of guilt pierces my gut at the idea of leaving Lonnie and Ida behind. But if I'm going to succeed at saving them, I know that first I must save myself.

I close the book I'm holding and return it to the shelf with others that contain essays on subterranean particles and the theory of evolution. There is nothing helpful here, but I've been through everything else.

"Raven, darling, you look lovely this morning," Titus says, breezing into the library and patting my head as though I am some lapdog.

"Thank you," I say, my skin crawling.

He goes to the large, ornately carved desk and begins riffling through drawers. "I heard you had lunch with Taylor the other day," he says.

I snatch a novel off the shelf in case he asks what I'm here for. I vaguely notice the title, *Moby Dick*, before I tuck it into my hands and answer him. "Yes. Brenna and Lacey stopped by afterward."

He finds what he's looking for—a small, metal object I've seen men use to clip cigars—and pockets it before looking up at me again. "How did it go?"

"It was great," I say warily, wondering where this is going.

"Yes, Brenna's father has already sent a note wishing you a speedy recovery, and Lacey's has offered the protection of the entire police force if it means keeping you safe. You've done well."

I recognize my opening. "Does that mean I'll be attending the party at Houten's tomorrow evening?"

His eyes gleam at my suggestion and I wonder if he's thinking of the building's layout, of all the weak points that provide easy access from an attacker. "I'm glad to see you're finally keeping up with your social calendar. Yes, an appearance at Houten's works nicely."

"With your permission, I'd like to shop for a new dress. It's what Raven would do," I add.

"It is, isn't it?" He purses his lips and I know he's weighing my poor start against my improved performances of the last few days. "Fine, but take Crawford. He seems to be marginally capable of keeping you safe. The others can follow behind just in case."

"I'll do that. Thank you." I work to hide my relief. Now that he's suggested bringing Linc, I won't have to. He's exactly who I need for this outing.

I wait while Titus summons Linc via text to meet me outside. "Go on, now." He waves an impatient hand. "I have work to do."

I rise slowly to my feet, pacing myself against the excitement at getting out. My steps are methodical as I wind around the circular hallway to the elevator. Downstairs in the lobby, my boots echo against the hard floor as I hurry toward fresh air. The doorman sees me coming. He tips his hat and offers a polite smile. I force myself to ignore him as I pass through and relish the feel of the air as it hits my face.

Three steps onto the sidewalk, I stop to wait for Linc, wrinkling my nose at the smell of exhaust.

A moment later, an engine sounds from behind, louder than the passing cars. It dies off as it reaches me and I turn. It's a motorcycle, shiny, black and familiar. I cannot see the rider's face through his helmet but I know him by the shape of his body. I think I would know him anywhere. Linc.

"You okay to take the motorcycle?" he asks over the sound of traffic.

"Absolutely."

I start to climb on, then glance over my shoulder at Rogen Tower. The windows feel like pupils, always watching. I pause, remembering that Raven Rogen doesn't shop on the back of a motorcycle. He looks at the building, as if guessing my reluctance. His hand rolls forward on the throttle and the engine revs. Throaty. Loud.

"Titus suggested the motorcycle," he adds. "More visibility."

"Of course." Still, my lips curve upward and I take the helmet he offers. When it's fastened, I slide in behind him, loving the way my body tingles where it touches his back. I slide my hands around his midsection.

"Where are we shopping?" he asks.

"Change of plans," I shout back. "Is there somewhere with no people around? No city?"

"Mother Nature in the raw? Of course."

"Will you take me there?"

He hesitates, then nods at the black SUV idling behind us. "Our escort will know you didn't shop."

"Can we do this without them?"

It's a gamble, asking him to do this for me. But even if he says no, I am confident Linc won't report it. Instead of shooting the idea down, Linc's hand pulls back on the throttle as his foot works the gears and we ease into traffic. "Hold on," is his only response.

And I do.

He veers left, then right, weaving in and out of traffic, missing bumpers by inches. I let it all blur together and revel in the way every heavy thought dissolves as we pick up speed. Wind rushes by and after a few moments, I feel a chill on my thighs. It is a comfortable cold, windy, freeing, and delicious.

In no time, we leave the black SUV behind amid an indistinguishable mass of chrome bumpers. Still, Linc doesn't slow.

The world flies by, but I keep my eyes open, taking in every turn and street sign. This will be my way out, and I need to commit it to memory.

Mount Vernon Square is a brick wall of brake lights but Linc never slows. I clutch tight around his ribs and suck in a breath. At the last second, we make a hard right onto Seventh Street, leaning until we're parallel with the blacktop.

While Linc weaves, I pay special attention to his movements and the gears under his feet. At first, it's nothing more than complicated twitches of feet and jerks and pulls of his hands, but slowly his feet and hands begin to match in rhythm. And I begin to make sense of the motorcycle's controls. Clutch in, shift, clutch out.

The city disappears gradually and the derelict buildings and cracked sidewalks give way to the muddy Potomac. Up ahead is the Francis Scott Key Bridge. Far in the distance to my left, I see thick forest. Between me and the trees, it is only open fields and deadened grass so tall I think it might cover my head.

We cross the bridge and it isn't long before Linc exits the main road in favor of more narrow back roads. The fields are smaller, the trees closer. Traffic is sparse.

In this moment, with the wind whipping my hair, the view endless and open, I experience joyful abandon for the first time in my existence. It is sweet and sharp. I want to memorize it, store it up, so that when I need it most, I can recall that this feeling does actually exist—and it is entirely worth living for.

On a particularly empty stretch of pavement, Linc slows the motorcycle and pulls onto the dirt shoulder. "Let's take a walk and stretch our legs," he says.

I slide my helmet off, hanging it on the bike where Linc shows me, and follow him into the grass. It is shorter here but still reaches above my waist. I wade in, and before long, the road and the motorcycle have disappeared behind us.

"This is beautiful," I say as we walk.

"It beats the city."

I tilt my head at him. "You don't like the city?"

"I don't like the extremes," he says after a moment.

I want to ask what he means but I don't dare tip the balance, risk him shutting down. Learning my way to the city's edge might've been my reason for coming but now that I'm here, reaching Linc feels just as important. "What *do* you like?" I ask instead.

His eyes clear and soften as he considers. "This." He spreads his arms out to indicate the scene around us before going on. "The taste of hot chocolate with marshmallows in it. A curvy road taken at high speeds. The feel of the throttle against my hand. The idea of home. My mother."

"All of that sounds lovely."

"And I like you," he says, and my heart stops. "Or, the you I get when we're out here." I think he can see my deepening blush, because he abruptly says, "What about you? What do you like?"

I weigh my words on my tongue. "I like the me that you get when we're out here," I begin, quietly. There's a risk to acknowledging his words, but I can't stop myself. His smile nudges me on, and for the first time in days, I indulge and answer as Ven. "I like silk sheets and the taste of warm honey. The wind on my face. Cobalt-blue skies that stretch beyond the horizon . . ."

"What else?"

I am still undecided on so many things; my list of likes is embarrassingly short. "Being here with you," I finish.

His head cocks sideways.

"What is it?" I ask.

"You didn't say family, or home."

I shrug. "I didn't say motorcycle, either. Doesn't mean it isn't on the list."

He chuckles.

"Your mother," I say. "You're . . . close?"

The laughter dies off and I'm immediately sorry for asking, but I want to know him, *need* to know him, this boy who would stand in front of a bullet for me.

"My father was killed in a protest three years ago." He wanders a few steps away. I stay where I am, giving him the space he needs. "Do you remember the backlash after the bill was passed halting low-income assistance?"

I nod. We watched the protests on the news back at Twig City.

"Suddenly, people no longer had enough to get by, and my dad had these big ideas . . ." He smiles fondly and then his face clouds over again as he continues. "It was supposed to be a peace march. No violence," he says. "The other protestors were like him, against weapons, against violence. They just wanted to be heard.

"They tried . . ." He squeezes his eyes shut against whatever memory is playing out behind his lids. When he opens them again, they're watery.

My breath catches, but still, I don't move.

"The march led them up and around to Pennsylvania Avenue. Then down and around to the National Mall. They wanted media coverage. They just wanted a voice, dammit." His hands fist at his sides, his eyes blazing against a villain neither of us can see. "At nightfall, they were ordered to disperse. Someone in the group became argumentative. The police came. There was a misunderstanding and a policeman was struck. When the officer got up, he drew his gun. My dad panicked and leapt in front of his fellow protestor. The officer took it as a move of aggression and fired. My father was killed instantly."

His silence is deafening. I have no idea what to say; I have no experience with loss of a loved one, loss of a parent. And Linc has lost both his dad and his brother. Very gently, I lay my hand on his arm. "I'm so sorry, Linc. He sounds like a beautiful person, giving himself to save someone else like that." He sounds like his sons.

His chin is steel and resolve as he nods once. "He was."

"And your mother?" I ask.

"The government gave her a settlement. She lives in a small apartment on the edge of downtown. She cooks for a congressman."

I turn to him. "But if your family received money from the government, why does she work?"

"Because even a sizable settlement isn't enough to live comfortably in the city. And if we can't afford that, the only places left are the outer edges and, well, you saw the luxury available there." His words twist with sarcasm but I know it is not directed at me. I can only imagine what he's been through, and though my own upbringing has occurred more or less inside the walls of a prison, I've wanted for nothing—or nothing material anyway.

My hand shakes where it still rests across his arm and I let it fall away. Where our skin touched, it tingles now. It's a delicious sort of wanting that I can never allow myself to satisfy. Not if I want to keep him safe, away from Titus's scrutiny. And he's lost so much already.

His arm twitches and then, as if by some magnetic mental force, his fingers creep across my palm and lace around mine. I flinch at the rush of being touched—and because I know I can't let it last.

"Linc . . ." I begin.

"It's just for a minute," he says quietly. "And then we'll go back to before."

I nod. "All right."

We stand this way for a few minutes. I don't move and barely breathe until Linc finally pulls away. Even then, I'm not sure what the right thing is. He's asking, without words, for so much more than I can give him.

"Let's walk," he says roughly.

It's not long before we come to the edge of the field. There is a wide lane of ankle-high wheatgrass before the woods encroach and take over. I stop and stare into the trees, my back to Linc.

When I turn back, Linc is watching me. "What is it?" I ask.

"Your hair is almost exactly the same color as the wheat."

I smile. "Ida used to say the same thing."

His expression changes from one of earnest interest to one of baffled curiosity.

"Who is Ida?" he asks. "I wasn't briefed on her."

"She is . . . someone I knew a long time ago," I say vaguely.

He steps closer, depressing the tall grass with his boots. "You used to be a much better liar."

I hear the demand in the statement. "I guess so," I say with a shrug and what I hope is nonchalance.

He searches my face. I know he is frustrated. "It's like you're a different person," he murmurs.

My heart clenches as if a fist has wrapped around it. For a terrifying second, I wonder if he's figured it out. But he still looks lost and disappointed, and I know that he's only speaking metaphorically. He has no idea it's possible, that his words could be literal.

"Well, I did almost die—"

"No," he interrupts. "It's more than that. I know there's something you're not telling me, Raven. I may only have worked here a few months, but I can see there's more going on than I'm being told. Not just with you, but Titus, Gus, all of them. Everything's a damned secret."

I flip my hair, giving him a heavy dose of Raven. "I don't know what you mean. Maybe you should ask your boss."

"I'm not asking him. I'm asking you," he snaps.

I can't think of an answer that will pacify him. "Seriously, Linc. A near-death experience can change a girl." I can hear my voice strain to remain light. "Maybe I want to live a little." I'm referring to the motorcycle. And him. But if he asks, I am prepared to say it's just the motorcycle.

"What about Daniel?" he shoots back instead. There's something I can't quite define in his eyes. Jealousy? "You didn't want to live a little with him?"

My hands ball into fists. "There are other ways to live besides hopping into bed with someone," I say furiously.

He shakes his head. "That's what I mean. The old you wouldn't have said that. The old you wouldn't have even thought it."

And because he's right and because there's nothing I can do about it, I'm furious. Furious at the real Raven for leaving, and furious at the rest of them for forcing me to be anything other than myself in front of the only Authentic I care about.

"Why do you think you know me so well?" I say, my voice growing louder. "You said yourself that we aren't even friends. This is just a job. So how do you all of a sudden know what I'm thinking?"

"I've spent enough time in the same room with you to witness how you choose to live. And none of it involves motorcycle rides, or turning down advances from guys with trust funds, or anything to do with me. You're not deep enough for these things. You're surface. You're Raven Rogen!"

"What is *that* supposed to mean?" I demand.

"You know exactly what it means. You're Titus's daughter. In every way. You care more about the shoes on your feet than the people you step on with them. Me included."

We are yelling, but I don't care. There's no one to hear and I hate that he's brought me all the way out here, confided in me, only to throw it all back in my face by reminding me who I am. Who I'm supposed to be.

"People change, deal with it," I say.

"No, they don't. Not like this, not this fast."

"Linc, I . . ." I have no idea what to say, but I desperately want to say something, because suddenly this boy matters very much. As does his opinion of me.

But his safety matters more.

"I don't know what makes you an expert on human psychology. You're nothing more than a glorified rent-a-cop," I snap at him.

He stills and I know I've hit a nerve.

"Fine. Just remember: Nothing stays secret forever." He turns on his heel.

Maybe not, I think as I follow him back to the motorcycle. *But by the time you figure out mine, I'll be long gone.*

CHAPTER FIFTEEN

THE NEXT EVENING, with Sofia's help, I pull on a floor-length navy gown with sleeves that come to just below my elbow. It is high-necked, so only an inch of bruising shows above the collar. I found it in the back of Raven's closet. The tags are still on. I cross my fingers that Titus has never seen it before and will think I bought it on my "shopping" trip with Linc.

"Does it work?" I ask her, adjusting the neckline.

She examines me and frowns. "We'll have to use makeup to cover the rest."

She grabs powder and concealer from the vanity. I stand still and try not to wince as she pats the cover-up onto my tender throat and jaw.

"There you are," she says quietly when she's finished. She spins me toward the mirror and I turn left and right to inspect her work. I barely recognize my reflection. Beneath heavily shaded lids, my eyes are hard, and my mouth is set in a determined frown. My eggplant-colored bruises have vanished in a trick of makeup, smoothing my skin.

"Amazing," I say. "Thank you."

Sofia smiles tightly. "Have fun tonight."

As soon as she leaves, I go to the dresser and remove the wad of money I swiped from Taylor. Two thousand dollars won't take me far, but if I can at least get clear of the city, I can game-plan from there.

A knock sounds. "Five minutes," Gus calls gruffly.

I stuff the money into the underside of my bra and adjust it until it's invisible through all the layers of fabric. After a final trip into my closet, I come away with the only other items I have room for—a pair of ballet flats for an easier getaway—and stuff them into the small clutch I'll carry. When everything is stowed and concealed, I slide my feet into a pair of nude heels.

Another rap jars the door. I pull it open, but stop short. It's not Gus waiting for me on the other side—it's Linc.

He's wearing a tuxedo without the jacket. His shoulders and chest fill out the white dress shirt, and the fabric pulls taut around his rib cage. His brown eyes glint in the dim hall. The effect is dangerously sexy. My breath catches and I completely forget for a moment what the next step in the plan is. Or that tonight, he's only a means to an end. I tell myself that using him won't make me like Raven. It will make me free. And it will keep him alive.

I watch as he takes in all of me. My pulse quickens. "How do I look?" I ask quietly.

"Do you really care what a rent-a-cop thinks?" he shoots back, but his words lack bite. We both know I only said it to distract from his demand for the truth.

"I'm sorry. I didn't mean . . . you're so much more . . . than that."

There's a heavy beat of silence. I hold his gaze until guilt gets the better of me. "So? The dress? Is it okay?" I ask, again glancing down at the lacy fabric.

His eyes drift downward once more.

"It is . . . more than okay," he says finally, his voice hoarse.

A thrill of pleasure courses through me. I smile, and for some reason, that's all it takes to break the spell. Linc clears his throat. "You ready?"

"Let's do it."

The house is empty as we make our way toward the elevator. "Where is everyone?"

"Titus and Gus already went on ahead. There's a second team downstairs."

"They got tired of waiting," I said with a rueful smile.

His mouth gives an amused twitch. "Maybe."

"Oh, can we take the motorcycle then?" I tell myself it's only to further my escape plans and not because I want to cuddle up against Linc one more time.

As he hits the button to call the elevator, Linc eyes my dress. "You want to take the motorcycle . . . in that?"

"Why not? It has a slit." I pull the fabric so the slit inches upward and stick my leg out.

His expression tightens. "I see," he says in a strained voice. "All right then. Come on."

I smile to myself as the elevator doors ding open and we step inside.

The party is held in a metal skyscraper with steel adornments that have been sculpted to look like tied ribbons where they meet and cross at the apex. Twisted metal glints in the moonlight as Linc rolls us to a stop underneath a canvassed overhang. We're right off the main entrance, street lamps casting wide arcs around our position. I hesitate.

"Wouldn't it be better to park away from the entrance traffic?" I ask, glad he can't see my face. "I would hate for one of these limo drivers to not see you and scratch the paint."

"Hmm."

I bite my lip while he thinks it over. A second later, the engine kicks on and Linc rolls back onto the street and around the corner to the alley. We execute a tight U-turn and parallel park halfway down the darkened lane. Farther down is a parking garage with dim lighting, attached to what must be Houten's. Mounted between the garage and our parking spot is a rusted fire escape.

"This better?" Linc asks over his shoulder.

"Sure." I shrug as if I didn't care either way and Linc silences the engine.

I slide off, careful with my dress as I straighten and smooth the silky fabric. Linc stows my helmet and jacket and is busy securing his own when Titus appears at the mouth of the alley. He beckons me with a slight jerk of his head.

"I'll see you inside," I tell Linc and make my way over.

There is hardness in the way Titus stares. My bravado fades the closer I get.

"What are you wearing?" he demands. "Raven doesn't dress like that."

"It's the only way to cover my bruises."

He glowers at me. "Future shopping trips are off limits if this is the sort of thing you choose; I'll have dresses sent to the house instead. And don't think I don't know about your joyride yesterday, either. I don't buy for a second that Deitrich and Tamlin just *happened* to lose you in traffic."

I remain silent, too terrified to argue.

But when he continues, it's nothing more than a scolding over my appearance. "I will have Josephine send you better cosmetics to conceal your bruises. Don't wear something like this again. For tonight, you will laugh and you will drink and you will flirt. You will be her and you will not forget who you are," he says. "Do you understand me?"

"I understand."

He walks off with Gus in tow. I watch them go, more determined than ever to see my plan succeed. Hopefully, after tonight, I will never have to be her again.

A doorman ushers me forward with a sweep of his hand. Stone-faced, I sweep past him.

The lobby is crowded with arrivals and coat-checkers. People waiting for their friends crane their necks to see out into the night, searching for a specific face that has yet to arrive. Someone knocks into me from behind. I wince and am driven sideways half a step.

"Oh, I'm so sorry, Raven—uh, Miss Rogen. My apologies."

I turn around and find myself face-to-face with a boy with dark hair and even darker eyes. His frame is slight and bony, decidedly feminine.

The contrast of his features against his creamy skin is all too familiar on this handsome stranger in a tailored suit. I know his face in an instant, though I've never seen it before.

It can't be . . .

This boy in front of me with porcelain skin and a singsong

voice—he is her. She is him. However impossible, this is Ida's Authentic.

"Are you all right?" he asks, peering at me.

The way his shoulders slouch inward makes him look small and afraid. Like her. That, more than anything, jolts me out of my shock.

"I'm fine," I assure him. "What's your name?"

"Obadiah Whitcomb. I'm so sorry for bumping you. It won't happen again. I swear I'll be more careful."

Obadiah. Ida. Does he know she exists for him? "It's fine, Obadiah, really. I'm not upset."

"You're not?" His eyes narrow in suspicion and I can see the faint hint of black liner around them. As if it's been washed off but only recently and not very well.

"No, of course not." I smile at him

He cocks his head. "I heard you had an accident. Did you sustain brain damage?"

I laugh and it's so foreign, I let it go on a beat too long just to savor the sound. "No brain damage. Just . . . more appreciative of life, I guess."

"Obadiah! I told you to get inside and mingle. You are not sitting on the sidelines for this one. Not again," a man snaps from across the foyer. His hair is peppered with gray and his face is pinched into a snarl that seems almost permanent. I recognize him from the tablet as the host this evening: Senator Whitcomb.

"On my way, Dad. I was just chatting with Ms. Rogen here." Obadiah puts emphasis on my name. His father tenses.

"Sorry, sir," I say, turning on the charm. "It's completely my fault for bumping Obadiah and then holding him up, making him talk to me."

The man looks momentarily baffled. "Right, well, when you're finished . . ." His words have lost their bite.

He retreats and Obadiah turns to me with the ghost of a smile. "Huh. Well, brain damage or not, having you around may be useful if it shuts my dad up."

"Hmm," I murmur distractedly, watching the senator wend his way through the crowd.

Obadiah tilts his head sideways at my expression. "What's wrong?"

I hesitate. Obadiah's father is the man Daniel and Titus spoke of, the one they are pressuring to swing the vote in their favor. The vote on banning the poor from this part of town. This is the man they will use as their puppet. If not . . .

"I've heard your father has been very successful in garnering support for his campaign," I say neutrally.

Obadiah grunts. "No thanks to me, I guess. He's made it pretty clear I only make his life in politics harder. Hence this stuffy suit and clean-cut do. Not my usual style."

"Not my style, either," I say, gesturing to my dress.

He gives me a once-over. "I know. But I like it better."

I smile. "Thanks. Nice eyeliner."

Obadiah grins. "Seriously, brain damage suits you."

"Come on. Let's get this stupid party over with." I hook an arm through his and let him lead me in.

We're in the ballroom less than thirty seconds before a boy approaches us. I recognize him from the tablet.

"Caine Rafferty," I mutter.

"Shameless player. Unapologetic asshole," Obadiah says as if repeating a mantra he's uttered many times before.

"Is that his official title?" I ask on a laugh.

"It's the unofficial official," he says. He smiles back but his eyes are narrowed and trained on Caine's approach.

I didn't need the tablet to tell me Caine is of past interest to Raven. They spent some time in a storage closet at an art gala a few months ago, and the look he gives me now is more intimate than I know what to do with. He is tall and light haired and has a cocky smile that is a little mean when it lands on Obadiah. I tighten my grip on my new friend and stand my ground.

"Hey, Rav, what's new?" Caine frowns at the neckline of my dress, clearly disappointed.

"Not much, Caine. What's new with you?" I say.

"Dance with me. It's been too long," he says, ignoring Obadiah entirely.

I force a flirtatious smile. "Let me make the rounds and then I'll find you."

Caine raises a blond brow. "You're turning down a dance?"

I feel eyes on me, and I see Titus across the floor, watching me with glaring interest. Knowing what the real Raven would do, I suppress a sigh and offer him my hand, sliding it free of Obadiah's.

"I'll find you later," I whisper to him as Caine leads me away.

The dance floor is mostly empty, yet Caine leads us to the very center and then wraps his arms around me and pulls my body tight against his. His hand immediately wanders south. His fingertips graze the small of my back and then lower still. I react, channeling both myself and *her* when I smack him on the arm and yank away.

"Caine, this is not the place or time." I leave what I hope is enough flirtatiousness in my voice to balance the anger.

"Then what is?" he whispers in my ear. "Name it, I'm there."

I scowl and step back, allowing more space between us when I reenter his hold. I don't answer the question and he merely laughs at my silence, as if my poutiness is something he's used to.

Obadiah watches worriedly from beside the bar. I spin again and lose him in the crowd, only to find Titus watching from another angle. He is locked in conversation with a man whose back is turned to me, but his eyes aren't on the man, they are on me. Knowing Titus needs a show, I swallow the bitterness in my throat and prepare to give it to him.

The next time Caine spins me, I twirl faster, tilting my head back in enjoyment, and let my dress flare out around me. I fall hard into the circle of his arms. The rough contact sends a tremor through my bruised body. To cover the pain, I pull him close and hang on tight. Caine takes it as an invitation, pulling me against him so that our bodies touch from chest to knees. We sway suggestively until the song ends.

The next hour is filled with dancing. Every song brings a new face cutting in, another body pressing to mine—and as I dance, I look for exits. There are seven in all, including a set of French doors that leads to a terrace. I narrow my options down to the three that are unguarded, though one with a sign marked Stairs above it seems like my best bet. It sits directly beside the door used by the buffet servers and the waiters peddling trays of champagne, separated by a partition. Even if someone spots me going that way, they'll wonder which door I chose and the decision will hopefully slow them down long enough for me to slip away.

I keep my eye on the clock across the room, knowing better than to try and slip out too early. The crowd needs a full dose of Raven before I can hope to wander anywhere unnoticed. Obadiah surfaces twice more throughout the evening. Both times, he has a clear drink in his hand but his eyes have glassed over by the second and I know it's not water. I shove it back, the temptation to go to him, to hug him once more before I leave. He's not Ida. Not really. Still, I watch him until he disappears in the crowd again.

Linc watches from the far wall, his lids lowered to unreadable slits. Even from here, I see the coiled tension of his body. His eyes track me, sending a chill down my spine. I look away, then disentangle myself from a protesting boy and exit the dance floor. *Showtime.*

I walk to the French doors that lead onto a patio and pass through the doorway into the crisp darkness. A few people stand about, mostly couples, taking in the view of the gardens below us. I wander as far away from them as I can, into a darkened corner where the white string lights don't quite reach. The thick railing is cold underneath my palms.

I've grown warm from the dancing. My hair is sticky and itchy against my neck. I pull it away, enjoying the air on my bare skin. My pulse races with what I'm about to do but it's fueling me, not shutting me down. Like on the motorcycle, it's a rush, an awakening. Still, for this to work, I need my shoulders to slump and tears to well in my eyes.

"I thought I told you to stay out of dark corners."

Right on time. I drop my hair and twist around, letting a single tear fall down my cheek. "Linc."

He lips turn down. "Raven, are you all right?"

The sound of her name grates on me. Somehow, it's worse coming from Linc's lips than anyone else's. I wish I could make him call me Ven just once before I go. It's a silly and impossible sort of wish.

"I'm fine," I say, allowing my voice to tremble slightly. It isn't a hard act. My muscles ache, my feet are numb, and if everything goes according to plan, this will be the last time I ever see Linc.

Linc's expression softens. I move in, and even though it's what I intended, it's a surprise when he opens his arms and welcomes my advance.

His arms come around me, pulling me against him until our bodies are pressed snugly together. I tuck my nose into the hollow space between his neck and chest and breathe him in.

I've never been held like this by a boy. Knowing my first experience is Linc sends a rush of heat through me and I press closer. My resolve almost crumbles. For a split second, I want desperately to stay right here forever. Protected inside the circle of his arms.

But I know that no matter what happens next, this moment will end, and life will resume. I can't go back to Rogen Tower.

With careful movements, I inch my hand into his coat pocket and retrieve his key. My breath catches as he shifts away. I am terrified he's caught me but instead of pushing me away, Linc's arms only slide down to encircle my waist.

He pulls back just enough that our eyes meet. We are face-to-face and the way he's looking at me, even in the darkness, sends my heart into overdrive. Those eyes are full of questions that I can't answer.

When he leans in, I tell myself I'm giving in purely as a distraction, a way to keep him from insisting on answers. But the moment our lips meet, I forget it all. The lies, the pretenses—none of it matters in comparison to the rush of blood and energy and feeling brought on by the pressure of Linc's mouth.

He moves hesitantly at first, as if asking permission to continue. I wrap my arms around his neck, letting my fingers run over the cropped edges of his hair, and hold on. *More, please!* In answer, his tongue traces a line along the edges of my lips. I shiver. My lips part and his tongue inside my mouth, the deliciously sweet and musky taste of him, is more satisfying than any food I've experienced.

"Linc," I breathe.

"Just for a moment," he whispers, like the day in the field. "Then we'll go back to before."

His hands grip my hips and then cradle my back, pulling me in close as his mouth moves more swiftly over mine. It's a tender dance, building gradually into a pressured, heated passion. Every single longing I've managed to contain these past weeks comes rushing up and out. I cling to him and meld my lips to his in a heady combination of greeting and farewell. He does the same with me. Even without knowing that I plan to escape, he holds me as if he may never have this chance again.

Between the tingly, explosiveness of his kiss and the welling of emotion brimming in my chest, I'm not prepared for the sensation overload. Tears threaten and I squeeze my eyes shut against their attempt to shake loose. One manages to find its way out, tracking a salty line down my cheek until it slips between our joined mouths.

The taste of it is enough to break the spell.

Linc breaks the kiss and steps back, letting his hands fall to his sides. The loss of his touch leaves a sharp ache on my skin. I hold his gaze, my chest heaving in time with his, and try to find words for what I've just experienced. But there are none. There is only the two of us slowly fading back to "before."

My breathing slows, but my voice is strained. "I need to get back inside. People will be looking for me." I square my shoulders and spin back toward the door.

He doesn't answer. He doesn't have to. He may not know it, but we've just said our good-bye.

CHAPTER SIXTEEN

INSIDE, THE PARTY is in full swing. Champagne flows freely and the music is fast and loud. I scan the room for Titus and find him locked in conversation with two men I recognize from earlier tonight. Politicians and financial investors. Hopefully, their mutual love of money and power will keep him occupied long enough.

Several people smile and attempt to capture my attention as I weave my way through the edges of the crowd. Brenna and Lacey stand near the bar, formidably beautiful in their cocktail dresses, an array of worshipers spread around them. I smile at them and avert my eyes like I don't notice their waves or gestures to "come here."

The key is sharp in my hand as I squeeze it against my palm.

When I reach the foyer, I glance around. A few partygoers wander this way but they are wrapped up in their own conversations. I sidestep around the partition and slip out the door into the stairwell.

The door clicks softly closed behind me and I blink as my

eyes adjust to the shadows. I zip open my purse and pull out the ballet flats I squeezed inside, slipping out of my heels and into them. Then I adjust my dress, sticking the motorcycle key next to the cash; I will need both hands free if tonight's escape is going to work.

The parking garage is two flights down and lets out in the alley where we parked, but I don't go that way. Security will be watching those exits, just like they are watching the front door. There is only one answer: the fire escape that snakes from the roof to the alley below.

It is fifteen flights up to the roof. I am winded when I reach the door marked Exit in glowing red letters. I pause to catch my breath, listening for sounds behind me, but there's no indication I am being followed. I shove the door open and step into the chilled air. It bites into me as I hike my skirt up and break into a run. Scanning side to side, I spot the ladder extending up and over the edge of the roof. My shoes pound out the rhythm of my heart as I race toward it. I toss my discarded heels and velvety clutch into a corner, hoping no one ever comes up here.

The climb down is painstakingly slow. I concentrate on keeping my movements sure as I put one tentative foot below the other.

When I finally reach the bottom, I am sweating and shaky from gripping the ladder. But then I spot the motorcycle shining in the half-moon's light near the mouth of the alley. I break into a grin and run for it. I don my helmet and jacket and then, with a jerk of my arm, rip the slit in my dress up to my waist and tie it into a knot. With legs free, I swing one over and settle myself onto the narrow seat. I wrap my hands around the handlebars and adrenaline fills my veins. Riding shotgun is one thing. Driving this monster is another.

I turn the key and hit the switch and the motorcycle revs to life. The engine vibrates beneath me, a delicious hum of energy and power. The gears are a little trickier. Even though I watched Linc do it on our rides, there's still a learning curve to finding the sweet spot where the clutch and the gas catch.

When I do inch forward, it's halting and jerky and I almost dump it twice before I hit the street. But then I find first gear and the engine catches and I am catapulted forward and away from the sparkling life of Raven Rogen.

The streets are crowded with town cars and darkly tinted SUVs, so I make a quick right toward the bridge Linc took the other day. I bleed into the constant flow of traffic and head north. When I pass the glassy image of the moon in the Reflecting Pool, I lean right and merge onto the freeway.

Exit signs advertise lettered street names, then streets named after numbers. I tuck in behind a compact car and up-shift to match speed. When I hit the bridge, I smile behind the anonymity of my helmet, relishing the wind against my limbs.

My side mirror glints with the headlights of a fast-approaching car in the lane behind me. I hit my blinker and maneuver out of the way, content to let them pass rather than outrun them. The car slows and changes lanes along with me, matching its speed to mine.

My fingers grip the handlebars like vises. I'm so busy watching my mirrors that I don't see the glowing red brake lights in front of me until it's almost too late.

I brake hard and swerve right with nothing more than a

glance at my blind spot. A car honks and I'm vaguely aware of the SUV merging with me, still behind me, still content to remain there. But there's no room to outrun it.

The car ahead of me brakes and I am forced to swerve a second time to avoid a collision. I yank inward on the brake lever and immediately let go again when the back tire locks up. There is a loud *snap!* and then a screech as the tire abruptly stops skidding and catches traction again.

Something metal and slim rips out from underneath the bike and is left behind me somewhere on the highway. I look down at the dashboard in dismay as the dials go from red-lined to zero. The engine, still running, has lost power. The motorcycle jerks underneath me and I wobble even as I continue to pull back on the throttle with no results. I'm losing speed and there's nowhere left to go.

I suck in a breath and veer right toward the emergency pull off and, beyond that, the guardrail. A car blares its horn as it swerves around my coasting. The motorcycle rolls as far right as I can go before the guardrail stops me. My foot fumbles and then flips the kickstand down. I lean the bike into a parked position and slide to my feet, staring at the taillights as they whip past and trying desperately not to panic. Pulling free of my helmet, I let it dangle in my hand while I think. My hair whips around me, stinging angrily against my cheek and neck. Cars roar by less than six feet away.

My eyes burn—from frustration and uncertainty. I'm caught between turning back and hitching a ride when I see headlights rolling up behind me.

It's the SUV.

The driver climbs out, dulled dress shoes crunching against the gravel as he approaches. At the sight of the familiar brown eyes and their flash of fury, I deflate. The helmet falls from my hands with a thud. All the hope I'd felt a moment ago, the thrill of the escape . . . every last bit of it trickles away.

The man in the SUV is Linc.

CHAPTER SEVENTEEN

LINC'S ANGER IS its own force, a magnet that both polarizes and pulls me in. I can't look away but I can't bring myself to walk directly into its path, either. I don't have to. He stomps closer until we're face-to-face. His nostrils flare, his chest heaves.

"Are you crazy?" he demands. "Or just stupid?"

Despite how I feel, my voice is calm when I snap back. "You almost ran me over the guardrail and I'm the crazy one?"

He ignores me, continuing his rant. "You must have a death wish. I mean, it's the only reasonable explanation, because otherwise you make absolutely no freaking sense."

"I never asked you to figure me out." My temper's rising in the wake of my embarrassment. I feel the heat creeping up my neck and I hate how I've botched this. This was my one chance and I didn't even make it ten miles.

"You're an unsolvable puzzle, believe me," Linc says.

For some reason, that makes me madder. My arms cross as he points at the useless motorcycle behind me. "You could have killed yourself on that thing!"

"Sorry to disappoint," I shoot back.

"I—wait, what?" He blinks. "I don't—You think I *want* you to die?" He throws up his hands and stomps in a circle. When he circles back, anger has been replaced by determination and something else I can't name. "I don't want you to die, you idiot. I want to protect you. To figure out what the heck is going on. And you keep shutting me out."

I press my lips together. "How did you find me?" I ask quietly.

He glares at me. We both know I'm dodging the real question.

"I'm a bodyguard, Raven. A trained protector. I know when someone's pickpocketing me." His words are soft to cushion the blow but it still sucks to realize how transparent I've been.

"I didn't just kiss you for the key," I say, because it's true and because I want to somehow make up for using him.

"I know. Me too."

My eyes narrow. "What do you mean 'you too'?"

"You think you're the only one with moves?" He looks pointedly at the padded space underneath my bra. "What are you hiding?"

When I stay silent, he reaches over and snags the corner of a twenty-dollar bill that's come loose enough to peek out of the bodice of my dress. A few more bills come with it, each of them carried off by the wind, before I manage to clamp my hand down and secure the stack against my chest.

"Stop it," I yell and jerk back.

Linc waves the single twenty he's managed to snag in the air. "What the hell are you doing with all this cash?"

I don't answer. I can't. There are not enough lies left.

"Look," he says, his shoulders sagging on a heavy sigh. "There's something you should know. No matter what, you wouldn't have gotten very far tonight."

"Why not?"

His lips press together in a hard line. For the first time, he takes note of the cars whizzing past a few feet away from where we stand. "Get in the car."

"I don't know if—"

"Please don't make me point out that you don't have a choice," he says. "Just get in the car so we can talk without all this noise."

I hesitate a second longer, mostly to feel defiant in the face of his command, and then I follow him to the SUV. Climbing inside, I finally remember how far I've hiked my dress before tying it off. I yank it down as I slide onto the seat but it doesn't do much good.

We sit in silence until he says, "Give me your arm."

"What? Why?"

"I'm not going to hurt you. Just give me your arm."

I hold my left arm out and he takes it, sliding his fingers up my forearm as if searching for something there. He squints and leans in, inspecting my skin underneath the glow of the streetlights. I do the same although I have no idea what I'm looking for.

"There. Do you see this scar?"

I lean in until our heads bump together. There, barely visible in the shadowed interior, is a tiny white line marring my skin. "That? I've had it forever."

He frowns, still cradling my arm in his hands. I tell myself it's not important how wonderful it feels having his hands on me. "You don't remember how you got it?" he asks.

I shake my head, searching his eyes for the answer. A gnawing feeling plays at the edges of my gut. Ida had a tiny scar on her shoulder, and she doesn't remember how she got it, either.

"No. Why?" I ask, my voice strained.

Linc sighs and lets go of my arm. I slide it away, wishing he'd held on a little longer. "Titus implanted a GPS tracker in you. He must've drugged you beforehand, but it's there, under your skin. It tracks your location down to the exact latitude and longitude. Our security team knows where you are at all times."

I stare at him, unmoving and silent while I try to understand the full implications of what he's saying. A tracker. With exact movement and location. Everywhere. Always.

Even right now.

Sighing, I ask, "Is there a way to turn it off?"

"The serum you were injected with last week did," he admits. "It jammed your signal for a few hours and knocked you out."

I think back to the expression on Josephine's face. She knew it. She had to. "That's why I was out for so long afterward?"

He nods grimly.

Running a hand through my hair, I let my gaze drift out the window. "There's no other way to block it?" I ask quietly.

"That's the only way I know." His words are kind. I wish they'd been angry. Temper is so much easier to react to than hopelessness.

Something seeps into my gut. Not fear. Resignation.

"Why does it matter so much? What are you running from? You've never seemed unhappy before," Linc asks. He's in my face again, searching for answers, as if his gaze alone can pull them from me.

The resignation is paralyzing, but more than that, I'm tired of the games. Linc doesn't deserve it.

"You wouldn't believe me if I told you," I whisper.

He leans in until we're almost nose to nose. His hands cradle both my cheeks, and his eyes are pleading. Begging. "Try me."

My resolve crumbles.

"Please, Raven."

And dissolves into a pile of dust.

"Linc, I—" The words stick in my throat.

"You can trust me. Truly."

I nod and make a decision. After this, there's no going back. And I know my choice isn't just between telling him the truth or holding on to it. I'm choosing something most Imitations would never dream of doing. I'm choosing to feel. And to maybe let someone else feel something for me.

His hands drop from my cheeks but one comes to rest on my arm. I don't move to take it but I don't shake it off, either. "How much do you know about what RogenCorp does?"

"Officially? They conduct scientific research for private companies through grants and donations," he says, eyeing me as if he thinks it's a trick question. "Why?"

"That's not all they do," I begin. "What you said the other day . . . you're right. I *am* a different person." I pause but he doesn't react. I suck in air and my lungs fill to bursting. When I exhale, with it comes a burst of words. Of truth. "My name is Ven and I am a DNA replica of the human Raven. I am an Imitation. A product." And then I deliver the killing blow. "I think the popular term is clone."

Linc retracts his hand and leans back.

There is no more air. Inside me. Inside this car. In the atmosphere.

A cacophony of emotions play like a strobe across his face. Shock, disbelief, curiosity, confusion. Maybe even horror.

"You're a . . . clone?"

A scream bubbles up in my chest but I shove it down and lock it in the box with all the others.

"Yes," I answer.

A full minute passes while he watches me, head tilted. His gaze is unfocused, distracted. He's trying to understand. I doubt he will.

"How?" he asks.

I give him the simplest answer I know. "Titus."

Very slowly, he leans toward me. Gently, he reaches up and lays his hand on my cheek. His fingers are warm and rough and tender all at once.

"Amazing."

Before I can decipher a sensible meaning behind his word, he is pulling me across the seat and into his arms so that I'm fitted against him. I sit frozen. Nothing about this moment makes sense.

Linc holds me a moment longer, no doubt processing my words into a more solid reality, before leaning back to face me. His hands trail down my arms until his fingers intertwine with my own. His thumb strokes the soft spot in the center of my palm.

"How many . . . Imitations are there?"

I shake my head. "I don't know. Thousands?"

His eyes widen and his thumb goes still. "There are thousands of *you*?"

I force myself to concentrate and try to explain. "Well, not me, exactly. I'm the only . . . Ven."

Slowly, he raises our joined hands to his lips and kisses my knuckles. "Ven," he repeats.

The sound of my name from his lips makes my insides flutter. I lean closer. On a soft sigh, I say, "I like it so much better when you call me that." His lips quirk upward on one side. A half smile. It gives me hope where moments ago I had none. "And I'm sorry I didn't tell you before. I couldn't."

His smile dims into something more serious, more sad. "You had a lot at stake."

"Not just me. Titus—if he knew I'd told you the truth, I don't know what he would do to you."

He huffs out a breath that sounds suspiciously like laughter. I eye him.

"What's funny about that?"

He shakes his head. "And here this whole time I thought *I* was the one protecting *you*."

His amusement, the easiness with which he accepts and dismisses it all, makes me angry. "This isn't funny. Nothing about it is funny. I just told you that I'm not human. I'm a manmade *product*." I spit the word, hating how it sounds but needing him to understand. "And you're sitting here laughing about something useless like who kept whom alive."

"That," he says, "is not useless."

"It is if we both end up dead for having this conversation."

"Not going to happen." His words are coated in steel. Linc's certainty over our fate is, in this moment, comforting, believable. I hope his faith extends beyond the confines of this car.

Linc glances out the windshield at the lifeless motorcycle and shakes his head. "I knew there was more going on, that I was being lied to, but I never imagined . . . And all of it right here in front of me . . ." He pauses. "Where did you live . . . before?"

I tell him everything. About Twig City. About how an Imitation is created to serve his or her Authentic in life and in death—but mostly death. About Lonnie and Ida and how much I miss them. I tell him about notes from Marla and how they are a written trigger for the end. My sudden departure. Meeting Titus. The words my attacker whispered.

When I am finished, we are both quiet for so long, the hum of the traffic outside becomes our soundtrack. It makes me think of the pipes. Of my friends.

I can't take it any longer. "Say something," I whisper.

"It's . . . unbelievable." There is malice in his tone that wasn't there before. A lump forms in my stomach, comprised of rejection.

"I want to hate him," he continues. "I mean, I do hate him. For being a tyrant and a dictator and for dangling you like bait. But he's also a genius. He creates . . . people."

"I'm not a person," I say. "I was manufactured."

He looks up at me sharply. His jaw is set. "Don't ever say that. You are more human than he is. It isn't *how* you're made, it's who you are."

I open my mouth, but then he leans forward and I feel his breath hit my mouth just before his lips do. Linc pulls me closer and I hang on tighter, clinging to the experience. I never thought I had the right to want this.

When our lips part, Linc regards me with a smile and even

though I feel the urge to smile back, I don't. There is one more thing left to be said. One more reason why he and I shouldn't be here together, solidifying our feelings. Sealing them with kisses.

I take a deep breath. "I can't stay here. I can't be *her*. Not even for you."

Linc is silent. I can see him working it out, trying to understand where this is going. "Do you trust me?" he asks.

My voice is thick with emotion when I respond with a quiet, "Yes."

He regards me for a long moment and then gives a slow nod. "All right. Then stop lying to me and stop making hasty decisions. You're lucky I found you before the others. Next time, I might not." I nod, agreeing to his terms. "As for these attacks, you have to let me do my job. Stay where I can see you, where I can reach you if something happens. At all times."

I hesitate. I wonder if he has any idea the enormity of what he's agreeing to when I say, "Deal."

"Good. We're going to figure this out." He presses his lips to my forehead and then draws me close, holding me against his chest. I can feel his chin propped gently on the top of my head.

"We'll get us out," I say but it comes out in a whispered question.

Linc looks down at me and the fierce determination gives way to a soft smile. "Yes. We'll get *us* out," he repeats.

Butterflies rage inside me. "He's more powerful than we are," I say. I hate my own pessimism but it's also truth.

"He's got a weakness. We'll find it." His jaw is set. A muscle flexes along his chin as he watches the traffic race by. He is beautiful in his strength, his commitment to good. And he is mine.

I cannot think of a better future than one forged with Linc Crawford.

CHAPTER EIGHTEEN

I CAN'T HELP that, on top of everything else, I'm concerned for the motorcycle.

"Will you be able to fix it?" I ask as Linc drives us back over the bridge toward home. Our joined hands lay on the center console between us. The moment our tires cross the invisible line that marks DC, my hand tightens in his. With or without Linc, I hate that I'm going back.

His mouth quirks. "That's what you're thinking about? My motorcycle?"

"It's a beautiful machine," I protest. "And it's easier to think about than . . . the rest."

"It is," he agrees. "It should be fine. Looked like you snapped the chain somehow. I've never actually seen that one done before." He glances sideways at me. "How was it? Driving it, I mean?"

I meet his eyes and can't help the excited smile that spreads over my face. "Amazing. Exhilarating. Scary."

Linc chuckles. "And all the other adjectives you left out." His laughter fades and he shakes his head.

"What?" I ask.

Staring ahead, he says, "You're just a junkie for danger. You can't escape it. No pun intended."

"Neither can you," I say.

He squeezes my hand. "Point taken. I guess you could say it's in our job descriptions."

I hesitate, for fear of resurrecting the wall between us, but I've already bared myself and it's only fair. "Why did you take this job, Linc? I mean, after what happened to Adam, I would think you'd want no part of this world."

His mouth dips into a deep frown, memory lines of grief. I wait. Patient and heartbroken for all he's been through. "I took this job because of Adam. Yes, he died protecting men who take that protection for granted. But still, Adam *believed* they deserved it. He believed in equality and the basic human right to live. And I was pissed beyond belief when it happened, but I knew I had two options. I could be bitter and become the very thing Adam fought against or I could become Adam. Believe what he believed. And maybe leave behind the lasting mark he tried so hard for."

I'm quiet as I ruminate over that. A lasting mark. What would that be like? To live beyond death, if only in the hearts of loved ones. It's contagious, the concept that death isn't really the end. I squeeze Linc's hand. "Your choice is beautiful. I hope you know you've already made a difference. Left a mark," I tell him.

My eyes are wet and shiny as I stare over at him. He smiles softly back. "And so have you."

Ten minutes later, Linc pulls up to Rogen Tower. I move toward the door reluctantly before I notice Linc hasn't moved. The engine still idles.

"You're not coming up?" I ask, suddenly terrified and lonely at the thought of doing this alone.

He shakes his head. "My orders were to retrieve you and drop you off. I'll be back as soon as I can," he assures me.

I bite my lip. "Titus knows I tried to leave."

"I reported back that someone was chasing you. He undoubtedly assumes it was the redhead. Just stick to that and you'll be fine. We'll get away, Ven, but I need time. We have to do this right."

I blink back tears. He needs me to be brave. I need me to be brave. "All right."

"You better get going. Gus is waiting in the lobby."

I twist around and catch sight of Gus watching us from the other side of the glass. His expression is neutral, giving nothing away, but I know better. He is an extension of Titus's eyes. I get out slowly and shut the door without a backward glance. There can be no evidence of this thing between us, not to any of them. Not if our plan is going to work.

As I cross to the door, I hear the SUV rev and pull away.

Gus is unsmiling but silent as he escorts me upstairs. By the time the elevator dings for the penthouse, my palms are sweating. The first thing I see when the doors open is Titus. He is leaning against the wall, his suit jacket off, his tie loose. His demeanor snaps to attention at the sight of me.

"Raven," he says, running a hand over his bald head. His gold ring glints in the light.

Gus nudges me from behind, driving me forward, and Titus steps in front of me, blocking my path.

"Care to explain what happened?" Titus asks.

"Someone came after me at the party, so I ran. Thankfully, Linc stopped them." I channel Lonnie and do my best to hold his stare.

"Liar!" He takes a step toward me and my shoulders go rigid. "Do not think for one second that I don't know what sort of nonsense you attempted tonight."

"I don't know what you—"

Without warning, his hand flies across my cheek and I am driven back. My shoulders hit first and then the back of my head thuds dully against the wall. I wince as my head pounds out an echo of the impact.

"You are a foolish girl!" he hisses. "Foolish for thinking you'd survive without me and foolish for thinking I'd give you the chance to try."

He is in my face now. I can feel his hot breath, taste the staleness that mingles with the scent of alcohol. My eyes are squeezed shut because I know that if I open them, moisture will escape, and I refuse to cry in front of him.

"You are lucky Linc was there to bring you back. If he wasn't, you'd only be getting what you deserve for betraying me. Betraying your purpose." Through my closed lids, his closeness is a wall of stuffy air and threats. I press my lips together to keep from making a sound, knowing any response will be interpreted as weakness.

"We had an agreement. You would be her in every way. You would abide by the terms or be removed," he says in a voice that isn't yelling but is much scarier. "And if you think that means you can go home to Twig City and back to your meaningless existence of tennis and cafeteria food, you are mistaken. Hear this," he whispers. "If you try again, I will end you."

My eyes open out of sheer disbelief. End? As in—

"Good," he says, nodding at my reaction. "Self-preservation is a part of your genetic coding after all."

I don't reply. My tongue is thick and heavy in my mouth, weighed down by all the meaningless pleas my mind is screaming. How can I give myself over to defeat now that I've finally found someone else to believe in my victory?

CHAPTER NINETEEN

THE NEXT MORNING, I'm inspecting the red welt Titus left on my cheek when Gus comes for me. "Get dressed. Mr. Rogen is waiting for you in the parlor." He leaves with a short click of the door.

I check my schedule. Swimming is first. I throw on a racerback suit and a cover-up, and slide into flip-flops. My hair is much easier to make presentable than my face, though I do my best to cover the red mark on my cheek with concealer.

When I enter the parlor, Titus is standing with his back to me, shoulders hunched as he stares into the fire. I take a deep breath, stamping out the automatic fear I feel at the sight of him.

I clear my throat and he turns. His eyes are clearer today than last night. Tiny lines appear at the edges, giving away his irritation.

"There's something I forgot to mention last night," he says.

My unease grows with every step he takes in my direction. He works at refastening the buttons on his jacket as he walks.

"What is it?" I ask. I can hear the timidity in my voice and I hate it.

He smooths down his jacket and adjusts his pockets, taking his time. He seems to enjoy the buildup.

"I know you're capable of pulling this off," he says finally. "You put on a good show last night. Dancing and laughing at those idiot boys. But you still slipped up. That *boy* is not acceptable for your circle."

"Who?" I can't help but ask. I am frozen—terrified he means Linc. That he saw us on the terrace.

"Obadiah Whitcomb."

Relief floods over me and I release a breath I didn't know I was holding. Titus scowls. "I mean it. He is not like us. He is not a part of your inner circle. You can't change that now."

I stick my chin out, determined to fight for this one. There isn't much I'll go against Titus for, but this is one thing I cannot stand to lose. Ida, Obadiah . . . a single, meaningful friendship. I will not give this up again. "He may have useful information," I say.

Titus's mouth tightens. "What sort of information?"

I shrug, like I couldn't care less. "I don't know yet but I heard you talking to Daniel about the senator and I thought maybe Obadiah would say something useful if I spent time with him. Besides, he's gullible and doesn't ask questions. If I slip and forget something he thinks I'm just being my usual flighty self."

"He believes you are her?"

"Yes."

I wait while he weighs my words. I can see him turning it over. For him, it is just a business transaction. For me, it is everything.

"Fine. But make sure you don't give up your inner circle. And don't mingle the two."

He means Taylor. And Daniel. Though the idea of spending more time alone with him makes my insides burn, it's the price I must pay for keeping Obadiah. I nod, struggling to feign indifference. "All right."

He takes a step toward the door and then whirls back. "Do not forget, I will be watching. I am *always* watching."

"I know," I say, unconsciously tracing the line of my scar.

He stalks out, slamming the door behind him. I flinch at the sharp sound, then the tension drains from my shoulders and my arms hang limp at my sides.

Gus shows me to a small swimming pool on the other side of the gym. I swim laps for what feels like hours, until the exhaustion is too much. I float on my back to rest but the guard who watches the gym calls out, "Keep swimming!"

Anger bubbles up. "Why don't you get down here and try it," I snap.

He glares but goes back to whatever game he's playing on his phone.

I gaze at the ceiling, my eyes burning from the chlorine, and drift, running my hands along the tiny white scar in my arm, trying to feel the equipment there. I will learn nothing, pruning myself in this pool. But I bet there's someone I can get answers from.

I wait until the guard is completely engrossed in his game. With measured movements I slide my left knee up and down the rough concrete edge beside me. The skin peels away layer by layer until a sharp sting and a hint of red signal that I've broken through. I scrape again—hard—for good measure. Then I move toward the stairs.

"Excuse me," I say a moment later. I stand up and water runs in rivulets down my face and chest. I paste a sultry smile on my lips. The guard turns to me and gawks. "I really need to see Josephine."

He clears his throat and blinks twice. "Uh, that's not possible. You have orders to stay at the pool."

I make my way up the steps and stand, dripping, in front of him. "Well, then, you'll have to get a first aid kit, because I really need someone to take a look at this." I stick my left leg out, revealing porcelain skin covered in water droplets that have run red.

The guard grimaces and steps back. "What happened?" he asks.

"I think I scraped the wall of the pool when I came up from that last set of laps." I gesture to my knee and then back at the pool.

"Huh," he grunts.

I use my most impatient expression. "Are you going to call her or not?"

The guard glances at my bloody knee. "Don't need to. She's in her office." He tosses a towel at me. I catch it in midair. "Come on then."

I fall into step behind him, suppressing a smile. It is becoming easier and easier to be Raven Rogen. But even scarier, I'm beginning to understand her.

I am dripping a trail of red by the time I enter Josephine's office. Her head snaps up from the clipboard she'd been studying. "My goodness, what happened?" she asks, startled.

"She scraped her leg in the pool," the guard says. "Can you take a look?"

"Of course." She rises, ushering me in and him out. "I'll call you when I'm finished."

He nods and leaves us alone.

"Come over here and sit down." At her direction, I sink onto the cot against the wall.

Josephine's examination is slow and silent. She produces a stack of towels from one of the cabinets along the wall and pats my leg dry until the wound itself is all that's left.

"Nothing more than scraped skin," she says quietly and goes to work on treating and bandaging it. "You probably didn't need to see me for this."

I don't bother to reply. She's right. I should've been more convincing.

When she's finished bandaging my knee, she tosses the towels aside. She stares at my cheek for a long time with tightly pressed lips before rolling away on her stool and making notes in a file on her desk. Then she comes back and her eyes roam over my chest and shoulders to the nearly faded bruises leftover from my attack.

"You look better. Mostly," she says. I snort.

Her tone softens. "I can let you rest in here with me instead of what they have you doing out there."

I lean my head back against the wall and sigh. "Thank you."

Josephine goes back to her paperwork.

"How are they?" I ask a few minutes later.

She looks up from her clipboard and smiles. "They are the same. They miss you."

"Did you give them my letter?"

She twirls her pen in her hand. "I did."

I hesitate. And then, because she's my only link left to them, I ask, "Will you give them another?"

"Of course."

She hands me pen and paper and I go to work. The message is trickier this time. We don't have symbols for the term GPS, but I do my best. They deserve to know. When I've said all I can, I fold the paper and hand it back.

Josephine sets it aside and goes back to her papers.

"Josephine, can I ask you something?"

I wait while she scribbles a few more notes. When she's finished, she slides the clipboard away and turns to face me. "Sure."

I take a deep breath, accepting the risk I'm about to take, and let it out on a rush of words. "It's about my tracker."

Josephine's eyes widen almost imperceptibly and she glances toward the door and then over to my arm. "Ven, I don't think we should—"

Her glance alone tells me she has the information I need. I drop my voice to a whisper and press on, speaking faster. "Just one question. Please."

"What is it?" she asks, sounding terrified to hear it.

"How do I remove it?"

Josephine's mouth tightens. "I—Ven, what you're asking is . . . impossible. I can't talk to you about this."

"Please, Josephine."

She squeezes her eyes shut and opens her mouth. "You can't. It's . . ."

I lean in, desperate to hear her answer. But before she can utter it, the knob engages and the door swings open. Gus steps inside and I straighten. He looks back and forth between us with a frown, clearly surprised to see me. I wonder briefly if the guard I tricked will get into trouble for bringing me here.

"What are you doing in here?" he asks.

"I scraped my leg." I point to the bandage on my knee as proof.

He eyes it, then me. "I need to speak to Josephine alone. You can return to your room now. I'll come get you for lunch."

I shoot Josephine a look but she doesn't meet my eyes. The cot squeaks as I push to my feet. Gus moves aside without a word to let me pass, and I slip out.

It's . . .

Impossible? Hard? Easy? Painful? A death sentence?

Josephine's reply, and the words she didn't have a chance to say, play havoc as I shower and change. No matter what the rest of her response would've been, it's clear she knows the answer to my question. But behind her uncertainty was a force I recognize well: stark fear. Someone or something has terrified her.

CHAPTER TWENTY

I DON'T SEE Titus for three days. Either Josephine worked a miracle and has given me time to heal before I'm thrown back to the wolves, or something has happened to draw Titus's attention elsewhere. The only silver lining to his absence is my time with Linc. He comes to my room most nights, although he doesn't stay long enough to risk being found. His promises of escape are a comfort but we're no closer to a plan or a way around my tracking device than we were when we started.

My reprieve ends on Tuesday evening, when I am summoned to what Gus refers to as "family dinner."

There are two people already seated at the dining table when I arrive. One is Titus. The other is Daniel Ryan. I've managed to avoid him for so many days I'd forgotten how unsettled our last encounter left me. For once, I welcome my role as Authentic Raven. It allows me to shove the fear aside and smile as if nothing else matters but pleasing these men.

"Good evening, Raven," Titus says as I take my seat.

I nod at them both. "Good evening, Father. Daniel."

"You look beautiful, as always," Daniel says, his eyes roaming over me lasciviously.

Sofia sets a plate of roasted venison in front of me and slips away. Underneath the table, Daniel's foot rubs against mine. I jerk back, glaring at him. He pretends not to notice.

"You've been hiding out," Daniel says to me. "You've missed three functions this week alone, darling. Is everything okay?"

Energy crackles off Titus but he remains silent. This is on me. "I've been busy catching up with the girls," I say, waving a dismissive hand like I can't be bothered to pin down my whereabouts.

"I see. Well, there's a party at Judge Strong's place this weekend. You should come." Daniel's gaze sweeps side to side to include both of us, and Titus shakes his head.

"You know I'll be tied up," he says, giving Daniel a pointed look that suggests something clandestine.

"Raven could go," Daniel points out. "The press always responds favorably to her appearances. And we could use that right now with the election coming up next week." It's Daniel's turn for a pointed look.

Titus dabs his napkin at the corners of his mouth before tucking the square of fabric back in his lap. "Not a bad idea. I'll think on it."

And just like that, the subject is closed. Sofia serves our meal and I take a dainty bite of my food from a heavy fork.

"This is divine," Daniel says around a mouthful of meat.

Titus mutters an agreement that is cut short as Gus appears beside him and whispers in his ear.

"Right now?" Titus asks. I watch the exchange intently, trying to decipher what's happening.

Gus whispers a response and worry lines form on Titus's forehead. Gus straightens and backs away.

"Excuse me for a moment." Titus sets his napkin aside and pushes back from his chair before following Gus out.

Something is wrong here. And I want to know what.

The minute I'm alone with Daniel, I take a bite of meat and fake a cough. Daniel frowns. "Are you all right?"

My eyes fill with crocodile tears as I shake my head and then nod. "I'm . . . fine." I down a gulp of water and resume coughing.

"Are you sure?" He looks more put out than anything.

I play up another dramatic cough. "Yeah." A tear escapes and runs down my cheek. I wipe it away in an overly obvious manner, making sure he notices.

Laying my own napkin aside, I take a steadying breath. "I'm going to freshen up. Be right back," I say, rising.

Daniel goes back to his own plate, unconcerned.

I slip into the hall, moving slowly until I'm sure no one's followed me. Then I quicken my pace. I pass by the library and three other rooms until I reach a heavy-looking mahogany door. So far during my time here it has remained closed, and I've come to know it as one of Titus's personal spaces.

The sound of voices coming from inside slows me and when I near the frame, I realize the door is cracked. Through the fraction of space, I see Titus speaking to someone whose back is to me. Gus stands behind Titus, ever the silent sentry, but his eyes are locked on the visitor. The scent of cigars wafts out the opening. I wrinkle my nose.

". . . But the RNA sequence is better than ever," Titus says. "These new models won't even have the ability to question their mission, much less care about their circumstances. They will be completely loyal."

"How long until they're ready to be woken and integrated?" the stranger asks.

"Six months, give or take."

"None too soon." The stranger's hair is wavy black and his voice is polished. "Twig City's beginning to look like a ghost town. We've depleted our numbers. Marla says the products are nervous."

"They'll be fine. Just keep them to their routine. Once the new line is introduced, their complacency will spill over and reassure the rest."

"That's what you said a year ago."

I can hear Titus losing patience as he snaps back. "I've done my best given the circumstances. Not to mention the timeline. You want miracles."

"Miracles are your specialty, aren't they?"

It's a challenge, even I recognize that. Titus doesn't respond directly. "It's under control," he says instead.

"That doesn't fix the problem with the current products in place," the man says without turning. He sounds unruffled, and I wonder if anyone has ever ignored Titus and his temper so blatantly.

"The current line is manageable," Titus argues. "I should think that would be obvious given Senator Ryan's replacement."

"For now," the stranger agrees. "Your daughter's product is another matter. And these disappearances are becoming disturbing in their frequency."

"We're getting close to neutralizing the threat," Titus says.

"What leads do you have?"

"Don't worry about leads. It's being handled," Titus retorts.

"Is it?" The man sounds angry now. "You have had more than one opportunity to catch her attackers. Instead, they've come much too close to taking her out, or worse, taking her alive. If that happens, they could go public and then everything crumbles."

"I will kill the product myself before I let that happen," Titus says, tone devoid of any emotion.

My body goes cold. I can feel the blood draining from my face. Titus whirls, heading directly for the door—and me huddled beside it. I run down the hall back to the dining room, but force myself to walk the last few steps. As I slip inside, I try to keep my breathing even and reclaim my seat.

Daniel looks up from his phone but only long enough to glance at me and shovel in another bite. He goes back to scrolling through the screen and I'm grateful that whatever he's reading is so interesting that it distracts his attention from me for once.

My hands shake as I grab my fork. Senator Ryan is an Imitation. Linc said his brother died in an attack but that the senator survived. Was he wrong about that? What happened to the Authentic Senator Ryan? And does Daniel know that his father is not his father?

They made it sound as if the senator isn't the only one Titus has switched out. The idea of so many more Imitations in place means the reach of Titus's control extends much further than I ever imagined.

I wonder who the strange man is and how he has the power to speak to Titus that way. And the more I try to shut it out, the louder Titus's words ring in my ears: *I will kill the product myself before I let that happen* . . .

He's hinted as much in the past but he's never said it like that, never with absolute conviction.

"Are you all right?" Daniel asks.

He's watching me. I force a dainty bite of venison into my mouth and chew methodically. "Fine," I say around the tasteless food.

His eyes narrow and he leans in. Before he can reply, Titus returns. He resumes his own meal, digging into the food with gusto. It takes him a moment to notice me. But I've fallen still again.

"Raven, you look pale," Titus says.

I force a smile and spear another bite with my fork. "I'm fine. I swallowed wrong earlier. But I'm much better now." I fill my mouth with food so that I'm saved from further explanation.

"I thought she was going to hack up a lung," Daniel adds, and it's enough of an explanation for Titus to let it go. While the two men resume their earlier debate over the misappropriations of medical research funding, I reel over all I've learned. I *need* to find a way out, but I promised Linc. For now, I have to stay.

Waiting for Linc that night wears me to shreds. By the time he slips into my room, I've demolished an entire pint of peach ice cream I found in Raven's mini-fridge. I finally understand the term "comfort food." No part of me wants to deliver this new truth about his brother, but I can't keep it from him, either. I remind myself it's not me who has destroyed lives—it is Titus and his quest for power. His thirst for creation and domination.

"You're here," I say, my relief pouring into the words.

He pushes the door closed behind him and his brows knit as he takes in my expression. "What happened?"

I tell him in a hushed voice about following Titus to his office.

"Ven, the cameras," he interrupts.

I shake my head. "The only one I passed by is pointed at the library. I edged along the far wall, so it missed me."

"And there's the one outside your bedroom," he adds.

My pride for my sleuthing skills deflates. "There's a camera outside my bedroom?"

"Relax. I flip it aside when I visit. You didn't go that way after you overheard them, did you?"

"No. I went back to dinner." I shudder at the memory of Daniel touching me underneath the table but I don't bring it up. There are more important things tonight. Instead, I finish telling him everything I overheard from Titus and the stranger.

Linc shakes his head, more in disgust than disbelief. "It was a cover-up. Adam died for a cover-up."

"I'm so sorry, Linc."

More silence. Lines crease his forehead and his lips are pressed thin. But more than that, his empty stare tells me it's only his body that's here in this room. His mind, his thoughts are somewhere else entirely.

Finally, he blinks and the fog clears. "Come here," he says quietly.

He leads me to the bed and pulls me down, sitting beside him so close that our legs press together from hip to knee. He wraps an arm around my shoulders, pressing his lips to my temple. "He's not going to kill you," he whispers as I lean against him.

"He's the creator, Linc. He can do whatever he wants."

He straightens and faces me. His determination is a lifeline. "No, he can't. Not to you. I just need some more time, okay? We're going to find a way to block your GPS and we're getting out of here. Together."

"You could inject me," I offer. "Like before."

"That was only temporary. We need something permanent."

My eyes light with an idea. "Josephine."

"What?"

"Josephine, the doctor. She knows about my tracker. I think I almost convinced her to talk to me on Saturday but we were interrupted."

Linc's brows draw down in a warning. "It's dangerous, involving her in this, Ven. We have to be careful."

I refuse to hear his worry. "Josephine will help. We can trust her," I say, taking one of his strong hands in mine.

Linc exhales and I know he wants to argue, but even he knows we're running low on options. "Fine . . . we'll give it a shot. But let me talk to her."

"She knows me better. She might—"

"They're always watching you," he interrupts. "It's too dangerous. Please."

I sigh. I've picked my battle already—and this isn't it. "All right," I agree.

His fingertips trace the edges of my face. "I will do whatever I have to if it means keeping you safe, Ven," he whispers.

The sound of my name from his lips is like an unexpected gift. I smile at him and his hand slips down behind my ear, cupping my neck and guiding me toward him. "I love when you say my name."

His lips brush over mine, featherlight and leaving behind a delicious tingle that sends my heart racing. I lean closer, searching for the pressure of his mouth.

Linc's hands are gentle as he lays me down against the lavender sheets. I snuggle closer until my lips are pressed against the smooth skin of his chest.

His tanned honey skin is warm underneath my mouth. I want to taste it, to kiss everywhere, to explore the sharp angles of his hips, the contour of his abdomen. Acting on some unknown instinct, I dot a trail of kisses from shoulder to shoulder.

Linc goes still beneath my lips. I pull away, certain I've done something wrong. "What is it? Do you want me to stop?"

His eyes shine with restrained pleasure. He smiles and pulls me in again, pushing up on his elbows so that his mouth hovers over mine. "I absolutely one-hundred percent don't ever want you to stop."

His lips brush mine, soft at first and then firmer, more insistent. The heat is a steamy thrill that has me squeezing my eyes shut and moving my hands up to his neck. His lips tease mine apart and his tongue brushes my own. I gasp. Linc deepens the kiss.

His hands rove over me, caressing and stroking through the fabric of my pajamas. "Linc . . ." I breathe against his mouth.

"Ven," he whispers in return.

At the sound of my name, my senses are captured. The rest of the world is forgotten. There is only this: Linc's mouth on mine, Linc's hands in my hair.

His mouth leaves mine to trail light kisses over my cheek. His movements are measured and careful and I know he's being gentle with me. My heart aches as it absorbs his affection and I tighten my arms around his neck.

It is overwhelming, this experience of physical affection. I don't dare open my eyes for fear they'll overflow with tears. For fear Linc will see them and stop touching me. All I can do is hold on and let it sweep me up and carry me off. I cling tighter, squeeze my eyes shut even harder, and try to breathe.

As I lie there, soaking in all of Linc, everything shifts. My world cracks, crumbles, and reassembles itself—with Linc at the center.

CHAPTER TWENTY-ONE

ON FRIDAY, TITUS sends me to the party Daniel mentioned, thrown by Brenna's father. Though he can't go, he says he trusts me, but I know the truth. The man from his study is impatient—and Titus needs to draw my attackers out, tonight. He orders Daniel to accompany me and Linc to drive.

"Be ready at seven," Titus adds before leaving with Gus.

Linc's left eye twitches, but otherwise he doesn't react to the order. I, however, am terrified. When I return to my room, Sofia is waiting. She holds up a sapphire gown that shimmers as she hangs it over the mirror.

"Wow, it's gorgeous," I say, running a hand over the fabric in appreciation.

"It's the latest from Jorge Estrada. Just came today," she says before disappearing into the bathroom. Water switches on and she bustles back and forth, fetching towels and various bottles of scented oil. A moment later, she ushers me into a bath that smells like freesia and lilies.

When I emerge from my room hours later, Titus is waiting

for me. He nods appreciatively at my dress. I have to admit, it is magnificent.

"Very nice," Titus says, and though it's probably meant to be a compliment I can't help but feel as if he's simply given me permission—not praise—to look like this.

"Tonight, Gus and the rest of the team will position themselves nearby. If anyone asks why they are not with you, say you have grown impatient of the guards' constant shadowing. Do you understand?"

"I will be alone in the building?" I can't help the nerves that are building in my stomach as I remember the last time I was caught alone.

"Your security team will be just outside if you need them. And Daniel will be there, as well as plenty of others willing to spend any amount of time you'll give them. You'll be fine." He leans down and lowers his voice and adds, "Just be *her*." He straightens and pats my cheek in a way that feels like a slap. "Your bruises have healed nicely. Let's not come home with new ones, all right?"

I am not sure if he means from an attack or from his own hand if I screw this up. Footsteps sound behind me, and I turn to find Gus and Linc.

"Have fun, darling," Titus says loudly enough for them to hear. Then he moves away to speak to Gus in a low voice. Beyond them, the elevator dings.

Linc joins me, closing the distance between us and whispering, "You look beautiful."

"Doesn't she?" a familiar voice chimes in from the entry.

Linc steps away but not before Daniel strolls into the room with a cocky smile.

173

"Hello, Raven," Daniel says, leaning in much closer than necessary. His breath hits my face. It smells like stale alcohol and artificial mint. He plants a kiss on my cheek that lingers too long.

I resist the urge to bat him away.

"Shall we go?" Daniel asks easily. He's either unconcerned by my stiffness or oblivious. I take the arm he offers and tug him toward the exit.

Linc moves to follow us out, keys gripped tightly in his hand. Daniel raises his hand to stop him. "No need. I brought my own car," Daniel tells him.

"I insist," Linc says through closed teeth. "Boss's orders."

Daniel frowns but doesn't argue.

Linc stands in the middle of the hall, glaring at us. I will the elevator to hurry.

"I think the color of that dress is the perfect contrast against your exquisite skin," Daniel says as he pulls me tighter against him. Behind us, Linc makes some noise I can't decipher. I don't dare turn. Daniel leans closer and pretends to lower his voice when, in fact, he makes it louder. "Although I wouldn't know for sure until you decide to show me less of the first and more of the second."

My shoulders tighten and Daniel laughs. The elevator arrives and the doors slide open. I pull away from him and step inside. Both boys follow, each one positioning himself near my hip. Daniel pushes in closer as the doors close.

Though he doesn't move during our descent, Linc's energy is palpable.

Daniel seems to enjoy it, though he doesn't say anything else quite as suggestive now that the three of us are alone. When the doors open, Daniel takes my arm and tucks it back inside his before stepping into the bright lights of the lobby. Behind me, Linc is a sculpture of jealousy, eyes blazing, muscles coiled as he follows us out.

The moment we're in the car, Daniel drops my arm and turns cold. I don't even bother to question it. I'm too relieved.

The car ride is silent. Daniel spends the entire time texting with someone.

"Who are you talking to?" I ask, mostly just to fill the silence.

"None of your business," he says without looking up.

I catch Linc's eye in the rearview and he grips the wheel tighter.

The sign at the turnoff labels our destination Washington Park Country Club. The long drive winds through the center of a sprawling lawn dotted with orange-and-white flags. In the gathering darkness, I spot a cluster of golf carts parked near a closed-off storage area. The main building is made of brick with white pillars in front. It is smaller than I'd imagined, or maybe it just looks that way against all the open space behind it.

When we pull to the curb, a doorman with a meaty hand opens my door and pulls me from the car. "Miss," he says simply.

I don't reply as Daniel files out behind me, shoving his phone into his pocket. He offers his arm, all charm once more. I take it, aware of the eyes on us as others arrive. With a slippery smile, Daniel escorts me up the steps and through the ornately carved wooden doors.

Inside, the party is already in full swing. It is a benefit for a local hospital, though everyone seems more concerned with drinking expensive champagne than raising money for the sick.

But at least I know Obadiah will be here—with the election in a few short days, his father has been making appearances at every event in town.

I crane my neck searching for him but I cannot see past a fast-approaching man in a black-and-white tux. I stifle a groan. Daniel smirks. "Rafferty. What the hell do you want?"

Caine takes my hand in his, bringing it to his lips for a kiss. "The night was such a waste until you arrived," he says.

"Careful, Rafferty. You might trip and fall over your own wit."

Caine pierces Daniel with a glare. "Let me know how the dance floor looks from the singles table."

I roll my eyes. "Boys," I say, with a fair amount of disdain and boredom. "Can we at least get in the door before you start fighting over me?"

My chastising works. They both frown and step back. I sweep past them and head for the dais where the politicians are holding their meet-and-greet. I shake hands with a few as I pass by, a smile pasted on my face. The boys are both close at my heels, whispering insults through plastic smiles. I spot Brenna near the far end of the receiving line, standing next to a robust man with a strange combed-over hairdo. She air-kisses me through the crowd, her freckles scrunching, and I return the gesture.

"Dance with me," Daniel commands, leading me out into the crowd without waiting for my answer. I tense the moment our bodies connect.

Across the swarm of bodies, Taylor sways in the arms of a much older man in a way that suggests they've moved that way before. She catches my eye, gestures to her date, and grins wickedly. I smile back with a shake of my head, and she spins away.

"It's a shame your bodyguards had to miss tonight," Daniel says.

I eye him, wondering if he noticed Linc's envy, but his expression is deceptively innocent. "They're nearby," I say carefully.

"Right, of course. I can see how important your safety must be to your father for him to guard you so closely."

My eyes narrow. "They're monitoring the party and will come if I need them."

"I'm sure they will. Especially that G.I. Joe of yours. A real hero, that one. Does he chew your food for you as well?"

"Shut up, Daniel," I say.

His jaw tics, though his smile remains frozen in place. To the rest of the crowd, he looks pleasant enough, but I don't miss the way he tightens his grip on me.

I am rigid with disgust by the time Obadiah taps him on the shoulder.

"May I cut in?" Obadiah asks.

"Yes," I breathe.

Daniel lets go, clearly annoyed. He gets three steps before a woman in her forties grabs him and drags him away.

Obadiah looks beautiful tonight in a soft charcoal suit and silk vest. He drapes one hand gently around my hip. The other hand settles into mine, firm and reassuring, and we begin to sway. I cling to him gratefully, glad Titus isn't here to see it.

"I was looking for you," I say.

He snorts. "From the center of the dance floor? Because I've been here for almost an hour and this is the only place I've seen you."

"I . . ." My response dies in my mouth as I see a familiar face buried far back in the crowd. I stop dancing but continue to hold Obadiah's hand. The pressure of it anchors me.

It is the only thing assuring me I haven't been transported back to Twig City.

Hers is a face I've seen a million times. Before I go to bed and moments after I wake each morning as we share our ritualistic greeting. She is Anna, the occupant of the bunk beside my own. And although I can only assume it is her Authentic staring back at me, the way her eyes lock onto mine from across the room suggests something else. Something more meaningful.

"Who is that?" I ask.

"Who?" Obadiah twists around, arching his back as he searches for the one who's caught my interest. "Oh, you mean Annalyn?" He turns back to me, his forehead wrinkling in thought. "I think her father's a statesman. Benner is the last name."

"Do you know her?"

"Not very well." The girl circles the outskirts of the crowd, still watching me. "But it looks like she knows you. Should we talk to her?"

My decision is instant. "Yes."

I don't wait to see if Obadiah follows me through the crowd. A growing sense of urgency propels me forward. I deftly slip around the bodies that stand between us. When I've almost reached her, Annalyn suddenly spins on her heel and retreats.

I increase my pace, almost running by the time she rounds the corner ahead of me. The ends of her long blond hair trail out behind her—the only evidence of the direction she's gone.

"She went into the ladies' room," Obadiah says from behind

me. He is panting as if even this small amount of exercise has winded him. "I'll have to wait here."

I hesitate. It's clear this girl wants me to follow her. Alone. "Maybe this isn't . . ."

"You came this far. You might as well see what she wants," he says. "Go on. I'll be right here." He's bent at the knees, sucking air.

I take a deep breath and walk inside.

The stalls are empty. I am confused and wondering if I somehow missed her quick exit. I am headed for the door when a hand closes over my shoulder and spins me around. I muffle a scream and come face-to-face with Annalyn. Or . . .

"Anna?"

"Shh!" She holds a finger to her lips and I notice a wound on the inside of her arm. It is scabbed over and fresh at the edges, marring the delicate skin below her elbow. I fall silent and stare at her cut flesh. "Not so loud; we don't know who could be listening."

"Are you Anna?" I whisper.

She nods. "Ven. It's me."

A hum sings through me, but I bite it back and study her. "Prove it."

Her expression softens until she is one-hundred-thousand percent the girl from the adjacent bunk. "Lonnie says to be brave," she says softly.

I gasp. "It's—It's really you. When did you get out?"

"Of Twig City?" She shrugs. "Last week."

I want to be strong but heat pricks my eyes, forcing me to blink. It's overwhelming to be with someone from Twig City, someone who really understands what it's like. "And Ida? Lonnie? How are they?"

"Ida's . . . she's having a hard time," Anna says quietly.

"But Josephine says she's doing fine."

Anna cocks her head, her brows knitting. "Well, Josephine's wrong. Or lying."

A tear slips out and I don't bother to wipe it until it's halfway down my cheek. I feel responsible, though it's not as if I had a choice in leaving.

"Lonnie does a good job distracting her, though. Some new music and movies came in just before I left."

"Do you—I mean, how are you doing with your . . . role?" I ask. I am unsure what to call it or what is expected of Anna. I don't imagine her circumstances are anything like my own, but I have no way of knowing.

"My role is a lie."

Something about her expression makes me nervous.

"How do you know about Relaxation?" I ask. It's the question that's haunted me since that last day, when I went to see Marla. "How did you know to warn me?"

Anna takes a deep breath and shifts back and forth in her heels. "My Examiner, Lynn," she says plainly.

"Wait. What?" Our Examiners never talked to us about Twig City, just about our Authentics.

"She had a breakdown in one of my surveillance sessions a few months ago and told me all sorts of stuff she wasn't supposed to," Anna tells me. "She'd been acting strange and sort of on edge for weeks before that. One day, she came for me at training time and let it slip they were planning to use me. My

Authentic, Annalyn, needed me and I was being prepped for assignment. But . . ." Her words trail off, her head tilting to the side.

"What, Anna? You have to tell me." I grasp her forearm, careful to avoid her wound.

Anna's eyes shift to the closed door behind my shoulder. It unnerves me but I force my attention to remain on her, willing her to answer me. "During that surveillance session, she got a text or an email. I don't know. All I know is she read something on her phone and then she lost it. Started raving about how RogenCorp is in the blackmail business and America is going to be a dictatorship soon enough."

Panic shoots through me. I drop Anna's arm. "What does that mean?" I ask.

Anna's voice grows hushed, uncertain. "Lynn said that Imitations and Authentics alike are being manipulated. She said the world order as anyone knows it is a lie, even the world Imitations know. Maintenance is mostly a myth . . . few Imitations get to go there after their assignment ends. Few actually get a second assignment, because they've found we're disobedient after the first one. Most of us just go straight to Relaxation. And Relaxation as we know it . . . well, that doesn't exist. It's this or—" She breaks off, regret flashing in her eyes.

"This or what, Anna?" I can feel my blood surging with alarm, but I have to know.

She closes her eyes, takes a breath, and slowly releases it.

"This or nothing. They put us into medically induced comas and use us for our organs. When we're all used up, they terminate us and toss us away."

The silence between us is like another voice, shouting our impending doom into nothingness.

"I'm sorry, Ven," she says quietly.

I swallow down my revulsion. I can't have this conversation. I can't even think about this. Not right now. There's more I need to know before I delve into the spiral of "what comes after."

"Your arm . . ." I trail off, unsure how to finish but desperately needing a subject change. "Was that your GPS?"

"It's gone," she says simply.

I shake my head. None of this makes sense. "How? Can you remove mine, too?"

Something subtle changes. "I didn't remove it on my own," she admits. "I had help."

"Who?" The knot in my stomach tightens.

"Don't get upset, okay, she won't hurt you. That wasn't supposed to happen. She's—"

Anna is cut off as the bathroom door opens and a girl walks in. Her red hair hangs loose down her back and she smirks when she sees me, a satisfied, confident sort of smile. It's the girl from the alley.

CHAPTER TWENTY-TWO

I SCREAM.

The sound is muffled by Anna's hand clamping over my mouth. She yanks me backward against her chest.

"Relax, Ven," the redhead says. "I'm not here to hurt you."

I don't believe her. I can't. Not after what she did to me. I struggle against Anna's hold. I can feel her arm loosening. Adrenaline powers through me and I yank sideways and then I am free. I barrel into the redhead with my shoulder, the force of it knocking her aside as I tumble out the restroom door.

The hallway is empty, Obadiah nowhere in sight. I shove the stairwell door open and hurry through. I have only a split second to decide up or down before I hear the door opening behind me. I race downward, my heels creating an echoing thump against the stairs. I kick them off, grab them, and keep going, my bare feet slapping against the concrete. The sound is drowned out by the redhead's pounding boots as she gives chase. At the bottom, I reach a door and race through too fast to read the sign above, shutting it quietly behind me.

A hallway stretches. Unmarked doors marred by peeling green paint line the hall. I race to the first and try the handle. Locked. Second, third, fourth—locked. The last two are unlocked and cracked open. I leave the first one cracked, hoping the redhead will assume I went the other way. Instead, I take the second door and close it softly behind me.

Blackness envelops me, and I blink into it, willing my eyes to adjust so I can move without tripping or calling attention. On the other side of the thin door, I hear heavy footsteps shuffle this way and that. I hold my breath and silently pray that the redhead will choose the other door.

The footsteps shuffle away. I let the breath go and feel a momentary relief.

Then I hear another set of footsteps squeaking down the hall. The door to the other room slams open again and I can just make out the redhead's voice. The second person responds to her, the voice male and annoyingly familiar.

Daniel. What the hell is Daniel doing here? I inch closer to the door and put my ear against it, their strained conversation just reaching me.

". . . wasn't the agreement," Daniel snaps.

"Obviously. Anna came on her own—"

"Annalyn," he interrupts. "I've told you over and over, you have to call them by their Authentic's name. One slipup is all it would take to bring this whole thing crashing down. Titus is going crazy over losing his products." My stomach hits the floor. That word. *Product.*

"Whatever," the girl mutters. "*Annalyn* broke protocol. She got excited seeing a familiar face. I had to haul ass to get here before our newest recruit did any real damage." Her tone is whiny and defensive.

There's a pause before he answers. "Are you saying you can't handle one measly little product?" My legs feel so shaky that I lean my weight—carefully, quietly—against the door. I've never liked Daniel, but this? He's clearly working with her, my attacker. And with Anna? Nothing makes sense.

"Please," she scoffs. "Stop worrying."

"As long as you keep screwing it up, I'll worry. Please tell me no one else saw you." He sounds almost as threatening as Titus.

"No one else saw me?"

"Melanie," he growls. "This is serious."

Melanie. Her name is Melanie.

She sighs. "There was a guy standing outside the bathroom when I got there. I handled it."

I stifle a gasp. Did they hurt Obadiah?

"What guy?" Daniel asks, an edge creeping in.

"Whitcomb, I think?"

"Father or son?"

I hear the sound of feet shuffling. "Son."

Daniel curses. His expensive shoes scuff against the concrete floor as he paces. "You can't hurt him."

"What's the big deal? We can just switch him out for his product."

"He doesn't have a product, not in the way you think."

"What does that mean? You told me—"

"Senator Whitcomb decided—ugh. Forget it. Just shut up. I can't talk about this right now. What did you do to him?"

"I only knocked him out. I don't even think he saw me."

I let out a breath I didn't know I'd been holding.

"You better hope so. Where'd you stash him?"

"In the coatroom. I still don't understand why we need Ven. We've got plenty of others."

"And you don't need to understand," he snaps at her. "You only need to follow orders. And you can barely do that. Where is Ven—*Raven*—now?"

Though they can't see me through the door, I instinctually crouch lower at the sound of my name.

"I don't know," Melanie says. "I lost her. Probably gone by now."

"I need to go wipe the security feed to make sure no one IDs either of us. No more screwups, Mel. I mean it. Get Annalyn under control. Next time I tell you to grab Raven, make it happen."

"It's not my fault. That freaking security guy is like a ninja," she says with a huff. "He keeps saving her ass."

Daniel grunts his agreement. "Linc Crawford is a problem."

I shift carefully, trying to relieve the pinpricks in my ankles from squatting so long.

"Can't you get him reassigned?" Melanie asks.

He draws out his words, speaking to her as if she's a toddler. "Not without tipping off Titus. It's hard enough getting Gus alone."

"What the hell good was it to switch Gus for his product if he can't help with stuff like this?"

What? My pulse thuds loudly in my ears. Gus is an Imitation?

"Because it gives us the inside track on Titus's whereabouts. I made sure he didn't come tonight, didn't I? And now it's all for nothing because you couldn't control one stupid product."

Melanie sounds repentant when she asks, "What next?"

"I'll figure how to deal with Crawford. Get the hell out of here and back to base. I'll find Ven. And no more showing up at social events. This was too risky."

"Yes, sir," she says, her words once again full of sarcasm. There's a long pause and I wish I could see through the door. Or maybe I don't. It sounds like they're . . . *kissing*?

Eventually, the footsteps thud away and up the stairs. I strain to hear, trying to decipher whether it's two sets of footsteps that retreat or just one. I count to one hundred before I straighten out of my crouch and stretch. My knees ache from being bent so long. I wait for blood flow to return to my feet, then slowly crack the door.

The door is shoved open so quickly that I have no time to react, and a hand closes over my wrist. I jerk away but it's not fast enough.

The light from the hallway spills into the darkened room and illuminates Daniel, forming a nightmarish silhouette. With a cruel smirk, he leans in and growls, "Gotcha."

CHAPTER TWENTY-THREE

"LET GO!"

I wrench free of his grasp and tumble backward, landing on my backside. A grunt escapes. Daniel looms over me, stepping into the darkness as he slams the door behind him. I press my palms to the dirty floor, scrambling to stand.

Daniel kicks my arm and I fall back to the ground. "Thanks for making this easier for me . . . Ven."

My muscles stiffen. It is the same voice he's used on me in our past interactions—seductively sweet and nauseatingly fake. Only now it's laced with his knowledge of who and what I am. "How long have you known?" I ask.

"Since our lunch at Fuego's. Raven Rogen—the real Raven Rogen—would never have talked to me that way."

My mouth twists in disdain. "That's what you're basing it on? Because you're not used to being told no?"

Instead of taking offense at my insult, he smiles his Cheshire cat smile and leans down to me, laying a patronizing hand on my shoulder. "You're not her, darling. You never will be."

"That's the nicest thing you've ever said to me." I recoil from his hand.

He lets it drop and his next words are a mild reproach. "I'm not the enemy here, Ven. Try to understand that."

I can only glare. "You're working with her. Melanie. Don't you know what she did to me?"

The accusation rolls off him. "I do. And even though you don't believe me, we're the good guys here. You should come willingly . . . but you'll come regardless."

"I'm not going anywhere with you," I seethe. I rise on shaky legs and try to keep my feet planted. "Why are you stealing Imitations?"

"I'm not *stealing* Imitations." At my look of confusion, he adds, "I'm liberating them."

I let out a sharp laugh.

"There's much more going on here than you know," he says, stepping toward me.

I back up and play the only card I have left. "I could say the same thing to you."

It works. Even in the dark, I can see his eyes narrow. The first hint of uncertainty shows through. "What is that supposed to mean?"

"How's your father?" I ask, feeling a semblance of control for the first time. It gives me a small measure of confidence.

A frown deepens the lines around his mouth, a stark contrast to the smile he wore just seconds ago. "Why do you ask?"

"So . . . he hasn't seemed off lately?"

"I wasn't aware you'd spent time with him lately." His tone is a warning.

I tread lightly. "I haven't. Not really. I'm just concerned. I know how important he is to you."

His eyes are slits, pointed knives. "What is that supposed to mean?"

My fear pumps wildly into my heartbeat. Fear for Gus. For Senator Ryan. The real one, wherever he is. "Come on. Senator Whitcomb isn't safe, but your dad is? Think about it."

"You're so full of it." He shakes his head, dismissing so easily the one piece of truth I know that can actually hurt him. "What? You think you can just say that and throw me off and I'll let you leave? Not happening."

He grips my arm almost violently. "Let's go."

I wince at the pressure he applies to my wrist. It's only half necessary. A large part of me is seriously debating joining him willingly. He's liberating Imitations? Suddenly, it's hard to tell who the villain is anymore. He yanks, but before my feet can comply the door bangs back open. We freeze.

Daniel squints at the backlit doorway and the figure outlined there. "Gus? Dammit, what are you doing here? You're supposed to be with Titus."

"Sorry," Gus mumbles. His shoulders sag and he doesn't quite meet my eyes. This is not the Gus I met outside of Marla's office. How did I not see it? "Crawford alerted us that Raven disappeared from the party. I tracked her GPS and came here as fast as I could, but he's not far behind me. I came to warn you, Titus knows—"

Gus cuts off as he's brusquely shoved aside. Through the door, I catch sight of a black suit—and a shiny, bald head.

"What the hell is going on here?" Titus demands from the head of the pack, security guards spilling into the room from behind him. He looks back and forth between Gus and Daniel in disbelief.

Gus and Daniel exchange a heated look, clearly deciding what their next move is, and then Gus steps in front of Titus, blocking him and the other guards from us. "Run!" he shouts. Daniel tightens his grip on my wrist and starts dragging me toward the back of the room. How does he think he'll get us out of here?

I never find out.

Before we can get more than a few steps away, Linc emerges from behind Titus and pushes past Gus. He lunges at Daniel, shoves him forcefully to the ground, and aims a terrifying punch at Daniel's gut. Before Daniel can finish groaning, Linc has him up again, his arms pinned behind his back.

Linc always manages to show up when I need him most. I'm so overwhelmed by the sight of him—saving me, once again—that I can barely breathe.

I'm frozen in the middle of this scene—Linc restraining Daniel on one side of me, two security guards holding back Gus on my other side, and Titus quietly assessing from his position at the door.

When he spots me, his gaze zeroes in and I can only imagine what he is thinking. "You," he says, pointing a finger at me. "Come with me."

"Titus—" I begin.

"Silence! We will talk about this in private," he snaps. "Crawford, stay with Ryan."

Titus rounds on Gus and stares down his nose at him. "And *you*. What do we do with you?"

With a burst of frantic energy, Gus rips free from both of his security guards and grabs a gun from one of their holsters. He backs away from all of us, pointing the gun alternatively at Titus and Daniel.

Titus sighs. "Don't be an idiot, Gus." He looks completely unafraid of the gun.

Daniel, still held back by Linc, has beads of sweat rolling down his face. "I trust you will remember who can offer you freedom, Gus," Daniel says softly.

"Sir," Gus says uncertainly.

I have no idea which one of them he's addressing.

We never find out.

With a tiny jerk of his right elbow, Gus goes limp. His shoulders sag and his knees buckle. As he crumples to the floor in an accordion heap, his eyes roll backward in his head. When he lands, face up, his pupils are aimed at the ceiling, frozen.

"No!" Daniel roars. He rips away from Linc and tries to rush toward Gus, but the two other guards are quickly at his elbows, holding him back. He strains against them, leaning toward Titus like a rabid dog.

I don't realize I've screamed until Linc has pulled me to him.

"Take him out the back," Titus says, eerily calm. A few of the guards move forward without a word and begin hefting a lifeless Gus into their arms. I watch them shuffle until my mind catches up with my voice.

"Wait! What just happened?" I demand. My gaze flits to Daniel, searching for some sort of explanation. But he's swearing heatedly at Titus, still trying to break free of his captors.

I swivel back to Titus. "What did you do?"

"Gus was no longer loyal to his assignment," he says. He slips something into his inside coat pocket too quickly for me to see what it is.

"What the hell does that mean?" I ask.

Titus ignores me and instead addresses the guards restraining Daniel. "Bind him. Take him back to Rogen Tower," he says, his expression disgustingly neutral and unaffected.

"Sir," Linc says. "He's high profile. People will notice if he's missing."

"I don't give a shit if the president himself puts out a missing persons report. Take him to Rogen Tower and put him in one of the rooms on the lower floor. We'll meet you there."

Two guards bind Daniel and lead him past me. Linc's lip curls in satisfaction as Daniel's head hangs in defeat.

When we're alone, Titus turns to me. "What happened?"

My thoughts are jumbled, still reeling from what happened to Gus, but I force myself to focus. Daniel and Melanie may not be the bad guys after all, and until I know for sure what they've been doing with the other Imitations, I am determined to be calculated in what I say to Titus. "He tried to take me," I say.

"Take you where?" he asks.

"I don't know. He mentioned others." I am careful to sound genuinely confused as I ask, "Are there other Imitations being taken?"

Contempt rolls off Titus like heat waves. I watch as he debates how much to tell me. There is a flash of a decision and then he answers me far too calmly. "There are some Imitations being targeted while on assignment, yes. After tonight, and in light of your—Raven's—attacks, it would seem Daniel is behind them. I have every intention of bringing every perpetrator involved to

justice. You'll be doing your friends a favor if you can help me."
Titus pauses, clearly doing some calculating of his own, deciding
what he needs to say to win my loyalty. "I have reason to believe
they've been terminating the stolen products." Liar.

But instead of calling him out, I nod as if we're on the same
side, and tell him what I know. "The redhead who attacked me
before came back for me tonight. She chased me down here and I
hid. I overheard her and Daniel talking about how they'd replaced
Gus so they could keep an eye on you and try to get to me."

"Tell me exactly what they said."

"Melanie—that's what Daniel called her—said she didn't
understand why they needed me if they already had so many
others. Daniel told her to take me anyway. She said she couldn't
because every time she tried, Linc was right there. She suggested
they get Gus to help remove Linc since they'd switched him out."

"The alley," Titus says as if it's all obvious to him now.

The alley. The night I was attacked.

They must have killed the real Gus that night. Titus is nodding and fitting all the pieces together as if it's all a game. All I
can think about is the way Gus fell into a limp puddle when Titus
walked in.

"What did you do to Gus?" I ask again, quietly.

"The same thing I will do to you if you cross me again," he
snaps, and I know he's not going to tell me any more than that.
"I need you to think back over the attempts on your life and tell
me if there's anything you can think of that will help us find this
Melanie girl," he says. "Anything she has said, people you've seen
her speak to, clues she might've given. Does she know about Twig
City?"

"I don't know."

"Anything else?"

And here it is. My moment. My opening to tell him about Anna. The one who said it was all a lie. The one who is in hiding with Melanie—and maybe others.

"Nothing I can think of," I say.

His gaze is piercing, holding me in place. "Are you sure about that?"

Lying, especially during an assignment, constitutes treason. After just witnessing Gus crumple, I should probably be more hesitant to commit such an unforgivable act. But I don't bat an eye as I tell him, from one liar to another, "I'm sure."

CHAPTER TWENTY-FOUR

ON SUNDAY, I run the track until I can't breathe and almost spill my lunch over the edge. I've been left alone with only a single guard inside the door waiting for me to tire.

I was housebound all day yesterday. I am not allowed to leave but neither am I forced into a public appearance or party. I exercise. I eat. I do everything I can to ignore the pulsing of the GPS switch embedded inside my skin. I still have no idea what happened to Gus. No one will tell me when I ask, and I can't stop thinking about how easy it was for Titus to somehow end him across a crowded room.

If faced with the choice again, I would let Daniel lead me away. His words replay in my mind so many times, they are imprinted on the inside of my eyelids: *I'm liberating them.*

Wherever Daniel has taken the missing Imitations, he's left them alive. It's more than I can say for Gus.

But now Titus has Daniel and surely Daniel will give up what he knows. Titus will find Anna and the other Imitations Daniel's hiding, GPS or not.

I pump my arms to fuel my stride. Each time my scar peeks into view, it taunts me.

The roof door opens and Linc steps out. Behind him, the spot where my guard stood is empty. "Want a partner?" he asks.

"Sure."

He doesn't bother stretching before he falls into step beside me. I resume my pace. The November breeze is chilly and biting where the open air meets the lip of the wall. It's refreshing. We run in silence for a while.

"You want to get out of here?" he asks.

He's looking at me funny, like I might suddenly break. It sets me on edge.

"Yeah," I tell him.

"Come on."

I grimace and glance down at my sweat-soaked tank. "I should probably shower first."

He shrugs. "We'll take the bike, let the wind dry us off. Let's just go."

I hesitate again. But it's Linc. And I won't refuse him. "All right."

No one stops us. The apartment is quiet but I know better than to think it's empty. They're all downstairs with Daniel. I don't like to imagine what is going on down there.

Linc is right. The wind is refreshing. But underneath it, there's a current of something I don't recognize. In the rigid set of his shoulders, as he pulls to the shoulder of the wheat fields, I finally realize: It's fear.

I hand him my helmet and jacket and wait while he hangs our gear on various parts of the bike. When he's finished, he takes my hand in his and leads me into the tall grasses.

"What is it?" I ask when we've walked far enough to conceal our identities to passersby.

"It's about Gus," he says and my stomach knots.

"Tell me."

"He's dead . . . and he isn't."

My brows knit. I wait for him to say something that makes sense.

He takes a deep breath as if bracing himself, lets it out slowly. "What Titus did to him the other night . . . there's more to your GPS, Ven. More than even I knew. God, this is unbelievable." He shifts as though he wants to walk away or pace, but he holds fast to my hand and keeps his feet planted.

"Please just tell me."

"Titus brought me in yesterday. He sat me down for debrief. I guess since I saw Gus die, he felt the need to explain. Anyway, he told me a little. About Imitations. About Gus. There was something inside of him, something inside his GPS that allowed Titus . . ." Linc trails off. I'm too horrified to urge him on. I already know what he's going to say. "He called it a 'kill switch.' Said every Imitation has one built into their GPS. He killed him with the push of a damn button, Ven. I'm sorry. I'm really, really sorry."

My eyes fill with tears. They stick there, on the brim of my lids, waiting. Something inside me sinks and is eventually swallowed by a pit deep in my gut. A single tear escapes despite my resistance. "What are you sorry for? It's not your fault."

"I don't know how to fix it. A kill switch? I have no idea how to counteract that, and I feel like I've gotten our hopes up for nothing."

"Our hopes? What do you—?"

He pulls something out of his pocket and sets it in my hand. It's a small black box with red buttons lining the narrow end. I turn it over and over in my palm but I can't figure it out. I look back at Linc.

"What is it?" I ask.

"It's a scrambler. Blocks your GPS location and scrambles the signal for as long as both pieces are on your body." His entire explanation is also an apology, and he adds, "But it doesn't mean jack now that we know about the kill switch. He told me yesterday that he can access it, detonate it, from anywhere."

I nod, numb.

"I'm sorry, Ven," he says again. The anguish in his voice rivals my own and I realize he's taking the loss completely on himself.

"Linc." I approach him slowly, as if he might spook and run at any second. He is rigid underneath my touch. I run my hands up his arms and settle them lightly against his chest. Every muscle underneath my fingertips feels coiled and ready for a fight. "You have to stop blaming yourself. I'm fine. I'm right here. Nothing that has happened is your fault. It's his. And we're going to beat him."

The fire in his eyes dims. "But how?" he asks.

It was an empty reassurance, but now, with him looking at me like that, I have to mean it. "Do you trust me?" I ask.

It's the same question he asked me on the night I told him the truth. His features relax. Not a smile but something close. "I trust you."

I exhale. "Good. I haven't had a chance to tell you about the rest of the party. I saw someone there. I think she might be able to help us."

"Who?"

"Her name is Anna. She found me the other night and we spoke in the bathroom. She's an Imitation, Linc. I knew her in Twig City. She escaped."

"Do you know how to find her again?" he asks urgently. "Now's our chance. With Titus wrapped up in interrogating Daniel and the security team running on autopilot—"

"No. But—" I hesitate. He won't like this next part; I don't, either. "She's working with Melanie."

"What? No. Absolutely not. She attacked you."

"I know," I say quickly, and because there's nothing else to add to that, I repeat it. "I know."

"We can find our own way," he insists.

I don't argue. I can't bear the look of defeat he wore earlier. Instead, I let him wrap his arms around me and pull me against him. When he lets me go, I hold out the scrambler.

"Keep it close," I say with a smile that I hope doesn't look forced. "With any luck, we'll be able to use it soon."

Linc leans in and kisses me lightly. "Thank you for having hope when I didn't," he says.

I kiss him back, lingering longer than he did. "You are my hope."

When we get back to Rogen Tower, Sofia is waiting for me at the elevator doors. "Where have you been?" she asks, glancing nervously between Linc and me.

"Out," I say simply.

She presses her lips together and grabs my wrist. "Well, now you need to be in." She pulls me down the hall toward my room.

Linc follows behind us. "Why? What's wrong?"

"Nothing if we hurry," Sofia throws over her shoulder. "They've been looking for you."

We round the corner and I am stopped short at the sight of a very alive-looking Gus standing before me in the hall.

Sofia looks distressed at being caught, but otherwise doesn't seem to realize she's looking at a dead man brought back to life.

Bile rises and I swallow it down. I am shocked into disbelief for a split second—until I remember what I am. Still, my surprise doesn't dissolve completely at the sight of another Imitation Gus. How many are there?

Gus frowns, his gaze flicking from Sofia to me and then, farther back, Linc. "Mr. Rogen has called a security briefing. You're late."

"I'm on my way," Linc says, stepping around me.

"And your dinner is getting cold," Gus says to me.

"Yes, sir," I mumble, unable to form more coherent words.

Gus nods once and heads back the way he came, toward the security tower. Linc slips by me, his eyes conveying all the apologies his words cannot. I remember what he said earlier. That Gus was dead . . . and wasn't. I understand now.

He has already been replaced.

CHAPTER TWENTY-FIVE

DINNER IS CUT short by a phone call.

"You can take it in the library," Sofia says, gesturing that I should follow the security guard standing in the doorway.

I get up and walk out, too surprised to care about my unfinished meal. During my time at Rogen Tower, I've never once received a phone call.

"Who is it?" I ask the security guard waiting in the open doorway. But like the one who led me here, he only shakes his head.

I sit in the rolling chair in front of the desk and hold the receiver to my ear. A buzz of background noise fills the speaker.

"Hello?"

"Raven? Is that you? God, finally," says the voice on the other end.

"Obadiah," I say. Relief washes over me. "How are you?"

"I'm fine." I can almost see him waving an impatient hand at me. "Listen, I have some information."

"What sort of information?"

His voice drops to a stage whisper. "What I need to tell you involves tracking down a certain mutual acquaintance," he says. "A bathroom acquaintance. We should talk in person."

Anna.

After the party, I'd almost given up on seeing her again. But if there is any chance at all of getting to the Imitations before Titus does, I have to do it.

What Obadiah's asking won't be easy. The apartment has been on lockdown since Friday night. But Linc's words echo: *Now's our chance.*

"I can meet you," I say.

We make plans to meet in the shopping district downtown at noon the following day. By then, I assure him—and myself—that I'll have found a way to get out of the apartment.

After the call, I ready myself for bed, not even bothering to attempt finishing what remains of my dinner. My nerves are strung too tight to even think about food; certain thoughts run on repeat through my mind:

Our downstairs storage room has been turned into a torture chamber and now houses society's most eligible bachelor—or what's left of him.

Gus is a copy of a copy . . . of a copy.

I am embedded with a switch that will end me with the single push of a button.

Obadiah will help me reach Anna and Melanie . . . and possibly freedom.

Sleep is accompanied by turbulent nightmares. In one, I stand in a room full of faces, all different versions of my own. The only one different is Ida, her dark hair a stark contrast in a crowd of white-blond. I am overjoyed to see her and to escape the sea of sameness, but when I tap her shoulder and she turns, her face changes and she, too, becomes me.

I wake sweating, heart pounding, and it is a long time before I drift off again.

The next morning, I am groggy and slow to wake. Sunlight streams through gauzy curtains, a cheery slant of yellow amidst a mental turmoil of gray clouds.

Through my half-cracked lids, I catch sight of someone standing across my room. Panic spears through me. It's Titus, come to tell me I'm no longer necessary. But when I blink to clear the cobwebs of sleep, I see that it's Linc. I force myself to relax and push up to my elbow, knocking the covers aside.

Linc turns at the sound of bedcovers rustling. "Good morning," he says with a small smile.

I return his smile with a faltering one of my own. He crosses the room and gathers me close, burying his face in my hair. I hug him back just as tightly, just as desperate.

"Hi," he says simply when he pulls back.

"Hi," I whisper. My heart thuds at our closeness and I take in every centimeter of his face and tuck away the memory for another time. The imperfection of his angled jaw and shadowed stubble is beautiful and enticing. I reach out to touch it, tentatively at first. When he doesn't pull away or argue, I run a confident hand over the scratchy surface of his jawline.

"I missed you," he says, leaning into my palm.

"It's been twelve hours," I tell him.

"I know."

My lips curve. "I missed you, too."

He grins back.

And even though I know it'll spoil his smile, I say, "I received a phone call last night."

"I know."

"How?" My hand drops away from his cheek. He catches it in his own and intertwines our fingers before letting them rest in his lap.

"I listened in," he says. "It's protocol. Someone had to and better me than someone who will report it back to Titus."

I huff, irritated I hadn't thought of that. "So you heard, then?"

"Yes, I heard."

"I need to get out this afternoon," I say. "If he found Anna . . . She's my way out, Linc. Daniel's insanity aside, Anna escaped. Free and clear. I think she'll help us."

"All right. I'll think of an excuse and try to convince Titus."

"I'm surprised they allowed the phone call," I say.

"It's just the one," he admits. "Taylor called earlier. I told her you were still sleeping."

"Thanks for that," I tell him.

Someone knocks sharply.

Linc springs to his feet and somehow is across the room before I can blink. He opens the door with all of the force and bravado of a detached security bot. Titus stands outside, staring Linc down.

I flip my hair to draw his attention away. "Good morning, Father."

Titus looks back and forth between us and I deliberately meet his gaze head-on. We cannot afford to look guilty right now.

My heart races and thumps double time. I wonder if he can

hear it in the silence but he zeroes in on Linc. "Crawford. What are you doing in here?" Titus asks him.

I hold my breath.

"Sir, Brasserie Restaurant called to confirm Raven's ticket for this coming weekend. They had her down for a plus one for the victory party but I changed it, considering we're detaining her latest boyfriend."

Titus frowns. "I forgot all about that. It's for Senator Whitcomb, isn't it?"

Though I am not surprised, I'm still disgusted they have a victory party planned so far ahead of time. The election isn't until tomorrow, but they're already certain.

"Yes, sir. It would be good for appearances if she went. We were just discussing a shopping trip this afternoon so that Raven can find a dress."

Titus stares at Linc and then nods thoughtfully. "Call them back and make her dinner reservation for a plus one."

"Sir?"

"You must accompany her at all times," Titus says, as if it's the most obvious thing in the world. "This Melanie girl is still out there and she will try again, especially when she discovers we have Daniel. It may even force her hand, a desperate move. We need to be ready. So far, you're the only one who has been there when Raven needed someone most. Can I count on you to continue to watch out for my daughter?"

"Absolutely, sir," Linc says.

"Good, then it's settled." He rounds on me, his features set in a warning. "And please select a dress that is . . . appropriate for your image."

"Of course," I tell him, plastic smile pasted on.

Titus grunts his approval, ending the conversation. "Crawford, I need to go over some things with you regarding our prisoner, but first I must speak with Raven alone."

Linc's hesitation is fleeting. If Titus notices, he ignores it and feigns patience. "Yes, sir. I'll be in the tower," Linc mutters.

When Linc is gone, I fold my hands, squeezing them together to hide my anxiety. This is the moment I've been dreading all day.

"We need to talk about Daniel," Titus begins. "I've spoken with him at length. He was reluctant at first but I convinced him to confide in me." I shudder at the thought of what he means by "convinced." "According to him, Melanie is hiding somewhere in this city with a group of my products. None of which seem to having a working GPS."

Hopefully that will delay him from finding them. Because if Titus finds the Imitations, it will be genocide.

"Those products are stolen property," he continues. "I want them back and you're going to help me find them."

My pulse jumps into my throat. No GPS also means no kill switch.

I hesitate, afraid to seem too eager. Truth is, I'll tell this man whatever he wants to hear if it means gaining another day in my search for freedom. "I will help you," I whisper.

"What's that? I couldn't quite hear you."

I force my voice louder, clearer. "I will help you."

His lips curve into a twisted smile that makes me want to kill him with my bare hands. "Good choice." He steps back. "We'll talk soon," he says before he walks out.

I glare at his retreating form.

* * *

Obadiah is late.

I am a mess, sweating, shifting back and forth as I wait on the balcony that overlooks the food court. Linc is out of sight somewhere behind me.

"Breathe," says Linc's voice in my ear. "In and out."

On the ride over, he fitted me with a device the size of my fingernail that he assured me would allow us to hear each other while he stays back to keep watch in case someone from Titus's security team shows up. I need to be prepared to play at being Raven, in case that happens. Now, Linc's voice is soft in my ear as he tries to talk me through my silent panic attack.

"He isn't here, Linc. Something happened," I say quietly. I stare down at the faces below me. None of them are the one I'm looking for. I check my watch again. Twenty minutes late. The knot in my chest tightens.

"I just called his house. He's not home so he's probably on his way now," Linc says.

"Right. Probably," I agree. Deep breath. In and out. "Unless he was intercepted," I say.

"We're going to give him a little longer before we think like that."

"Fine."

Three minutes pass during which time I check my watch no fewer than fourteen times. It feels like three years.

I almost don't recognize Obadiah when he enters the atrium. His jacket collar is pulled up to his chin and he has a dark hat tipped downward obscuring his face. But I catch a glimpse of his delicate cheeks, his narrow chin.

"He's here!" I skip the elevator and make my way down the stairs. Linc's voice in my ear reminds me to slow down, that I cannot draw attention.

I reach Obadiah at the edges of the seating area. I put my hand on his and he squeals and grabs his chest. "Do not sneak up on me like that!" he hisses.

"Sorry. I was beginning to worry."

"I had to double back a few times and make sure I wasn't followed."

That reawakens my anxiety. "Why would you be followed?"

He gives me a pointed look. "I have so much to tell you."

He takes my hand and leads me away from the food court. I let him, knowing Linc is close and hearing everything. If we are being followed, he will know and warn me. My earpiece chirps as we push through the door to the parking garage. "Keep going. You're doing fine. I'm right on your tail," Linc says.

Obadiah pauses, looks right and left, then darts forward, still pulling on my hand. He leads me in a zigzagging pattern to the far end of the covered garage and then opens the door to an over-sized sedan the color of mint ice cream.

"Get in," he says.

I navigate over the console into the passenger seat and wait while Obadiah climbs in behind me and slams the door. He winces at the sound and then turns to me. I notice dark circles under his eyes that have nothing to do with eyeliner. "I don't think I've been spotted but I can't be sure. How much time do you have?"

"Not long," Linc answers in my ear.

"Um, an hour?" I say.

Obadiah buckles up. "Okay, let's drive."

He turns the key and the engine roars to life. It is loud, unlike any vehicle I've been inside, and I stare at the dashboard as it reverberates with the growl of the engine. "Where did you get this car?" I ask.

"My security guy's cousin. It's vintage. Don't mock." Obadiah reverses and pulls left, down the slanting loop that will take us out of the garage.

"Where are we going?"

"Nowhere," Obadiah says with a shrug. "I just want to keep moving. In case."

"In case what?"

"Remember your daughter-of-a-statesman stalker from the party last week?"

"Yes."

"Well, I don't know what sort of scam she's pulling but I checked, and that girl died like a week ago. So she's either a really badass apparition or she's scamming."

"Scamming who?"

"That's the million-dollar question. Fast-forward to yesterday and I'm coming out of a shop in the west end and I see her."

"See who?"

"Dead girl. Annalyn. Only she doesn't look very dead to me. Or very apparitiony. So I followed her."

I stare at Obadiah, partly worried, partly awed. Ida would never have the guts to do something so dangerous alone. "Where did she go?"

"Not to her swanky home, I'll tell you that. I followed her toward the outskirts and, well, a senator's son can't exactly waltz through that part of town."

I picture the dilapidated buildings, the vacant stares of the sidewalk residents, and I know that he isn't wrong. Walking down there wouldn't be safe. "What about Anna? No one messed with her?"

"Nope. It was weird. They barely noticed her. Almost as if they knew her." He hits the blinker and we make a turn.

How strange. "You think she's been there before?"

"She lives there," he says, glancing at me, then back at the road.

I stare at him, surprised. "What? How do you know?"

There is hesitation in his voice the size of a brick wall. "Because the redhead told me?"

"You spoke to *Melanie*?"

"Relax, nothing happened." He looks over at me as we idle at a red light and pokes himself in the ribs. "See? Still here. Still in one piece."

I sigh. "Tell me what happened."

The light turns green. The car rumbles as he depresses the pedal and barrels forward.

"First, it must be said that I could've spied successfully if I'd wanted to. I just didn't want to."

"Obadiah." My tone is a warning.

"She caught me following Annalyn," he admits.

"And by 'caught,' you mean . . . ?"

He purses his lips and then says, "Tackled from behind and after much struggling where I had mostly the upper hand . . . she detained me."

"She could've hurt you—again!" I shout, my voice verging on hysterical.

"Right, but she didn't. We had an interesting talk, actually."

He isn't looking at me when he says it and I can't stop my mind from racing. What does he know? What has she told him about the Imitations? About me?

"What did you two talk about?" I ask, trying for nonchalant.

His eyes narrow and I know what he's thinking. I'm not fooling him. "She wants to meet with you."

"What?" Could it really be that easy? I thought I'd have to comb the city, dangle myself once more in order to draw her out.

"She said she knows you have Daniel—"

"How does she know that?"

He cuts me a sharp look. "Maybe the same way you know her name?"

I scowl. "What else did she say?"

"She knows Daniel's been found out, that she's next on the hit list."

"What hit list?"

After a long pause, he says, "She said she knows they'll come after her next."

I can't argue that. Even if Titus didn't want her, I do. Or at least the information she holds.

"When can I meet with her?" I ask.

I can hear Linc groan into my earpiece. For once, I'm glad he's not here. His arguments would only slow things. He might think Melanie's a loose cannon, but I have to know what she knows. If she can remove my GPS, if she can lead me to the others, it's worth it.

"She said you can find her at the same place I did, but only until the end of today. And don't come expecting Annalyn or any *others*, as she puts it." He uses one hand to air-quote the word. "I have no idea what that means but she said you would. You'll get to see them after you've talked and she knows she can trust you."

I snort. Trust *me*?

"What does she get out of it?" I ask.

He shrugs, both hands back on the wheel. "And therein lies the mystery. She wouldn't say."

"What's the address of the place where you found her?" I ask.

"Six-eighteen Garfield Avenue," he rattles off. Then his eyes widen. "But that area is so sketchy, you can't go there alone. Promise me you won't do anything crazy like that," Obadiah adds.

"I promise." *Nothing like that. Just your ordinary brand of crazy from here on out.*

Obadiah makes a left turn. From here, I can see the parking structure and beyond that the shopping mall. We're back.

"Obadiah, you'll be careful, right? This situation, it's dangerous—"

"Don't you worry about me. My spying days are behind me." He gives a rueful smile. "Sort of a one-and-done experience, if you know what I mean." He pulls into a parking space and cuts the engine.

I lay my hand over his. "Thank you."

He scowls. "Don't do that."

"Do what?"

"Act all nice and appreciative. I know there's something you're not telling me so I want to make it clear: I did this for you so you owe me. And I will collect."

Nothing about Obadiah is remotely sinister or scary. However, the prospect of telling the truth *is*. I can't refuse now, not after everything he's done. But I intend to prolong his unawareness as long as possible. There is safety in not knowing. "Deal," I say finally.

He breaks into a smile, as if he knows he's just won something huge. "Deal," he echoes.

CHAPTER TWENTY-SIX

THE WAREHOUSE ON Garfield is a shell. Businesses on both sides of the street are abandoned and windowless, most of them missing walls and some even doors. It's as if someone took a wrecking ball and went at it. The gray concrete offers shadows and too many hiding places as we creep along, searching for a place to tuck our security-issued SUV.

"You're sure my GPS signal won't give us away?" I ask for the third time. It's the only thing we talked about on the drive over. The tension inside the car is thick.

"Positive. I rerouted you to the downtown shopping district, near Mia's café, but we don't have long," Linc said, pulling into a tight space between a shed and a large electrical box. A large tree rises over the hood, its gnarled branches devoid of leaves and reminding me of the metal sculptured tree attached to Rogen-Corp.

Titus's symbol of science. My symbol of captivity.

I unhook my seat belt. "Let's get this done quickly then."

"Ven, wait." Linc's hand wraps around my wrist, halting my

efforts. His eyes flash a warning. "If we're really going to do this, you have to listen to what I say. Follow my lead."

"Melanie won't hurt me with you around," I assure him.

In all of this, I have come to realize one thing: In order to save myself, I must save the others—and Melanie is the only one who can get me to them.

Linc leans over and plants a quick kiss on my mouth and then releases me. We exit the car at the same time, careful not to let our doors slam, and approach the warehouse.

The front door is missing. A main hall runs straight back before disappearing in thick shadows. A layer of dust coats the concrete floors, seemingly undisturbed. My mind conjures images of cloaked minions ready to pounce. Linc peeks in and looks left and then right without letting go of my hand. We don't move from the entrance.

"Melanie," he calls out in a voice just short of yelling. "We're here. We've come to talk. Show yourself."

Silence.

Beside me, Linc is rigid. I am wound just as tight. My breaths are shallow, even my lungs scared to make noise.

"Melanie," Linc calls again.

From inside the warehouse, somewhere I can't see, footsteps sound. Not clicking heels. Boots. Lightly treading.

"Relax," I hear as a mane of red hair materializes from around the vacant door frame. "I'm here."

"Melanie." Everything in me wants to take a giant step backward at the sight of her piercing gray eyes. But I don't. We've come too far to run away. And I'm not facing her on my own

216

anymore. I squeeze Linc's hand until my fingers hurt and stand my ground.

Her lips quirk upward as she watches me. "I'm glad you came, Ven. Are we alone?" she asks pointedly.

I jut my chin forward, daring her to argue. "Linc stays."

She shrugs. "It's cool, I figured as much. When I say alone, I mean without Titus." She gestures around us. "I need to be somewhere he can't reach."

Linc holds his hand out, revealing the GPS scrambler he's carrying. "Titus doesn't know where she is right now, if that's what you're asking," he says.

Melanie's brow lifts, revealing her approval. "Good dog," she says.

Linc glares and opens his mouth. I lay a hand against his chest and cut him off. "Titus may not know where we are, but we still don't have a single reason to trust you. You have five minutes. I don't owe you anything."

She takes a step forward. I tense and Linc steps between us, blocking me. "Stay where you are," he tells her.

She holds up her hands in surrender or agreement. I look away; her hands remind me she's so much stronger than she looks. I am reminded of Lonnie, her wiry strength and unswerving determination when she sets a goal. I realize their jawlines curve in the same way.

"I won't move," she says, her tone full of innocence. I can't tell if she's lying.

"Talk," I say.

"Here's the thing. I know who you are, Ven from Twig City.

And I know what you are: an Imitation, grown from a test tube. I know there is an entire warehouse full of you. Well, not you, exactly, but products." She pauses, possibly to let the full weight of her words settle around us.

"Daniel told me everything," she explains.

I put all of Authentic Raven's condescension and uncaring into my voice when I say, "You brought me all the way out here to rub it in that you know my secret?"

"No. I brought you out here to tell you I can get you to the other Imitations. I know where they are."

My eyes narrow. "They are there . . . willingly? And you're helping them?"

Pieces are falling into place, even before she answers with a definitive, "Yes."

"Why?" I ask.

"Because they don't deserve to be used this way. Neither do you, though I'm sure you'll find that sort of maddening coming from me. You might distrust me for what I did to you, but even you have to admit that I'm tame compared to someone like Titus."

I can't argue with that. I'm not ready to agree with her, either.

"They call you products, but you are people," she adds.

Nothing she could've said would surprise me more. "You don't know what you're talking about."

"No, *you* don't. The science it takes to create you . . ." She shakes her head. "You might not have been born from a human womb, Ven, but you're human in every sense of the term. Making you believe otherwise is part of the lie."

Linc is quiet beside me. "How do you know all of this?" I demand.

"Daniel. The others . . . and I've seen it."

She's being frustratingly obtuse. "Seen what?"

"The data. The conclusive evidence of testing that proves you have just as much emotion and ability to feel and experience as we do. Isn't that what you think separates you? Isn't that what they tell you? Humans are superior—intellectually and emotionally?"

"You've . . ." I don't realize I've taken a step forward until Linc's hand on my arm gently pulls me back. "How is that possible?"

Melanie folds her arms and her lids lower. "I can't tell you that. I've already sold Daniel out by telling you this much." Her voice drops to a mumble when she says, "I won't do it to anyone else."

I wonder vaguely who else there is left to betray. "How can you care what Daniel thinks of you? He only thinks of the Imitations as a tool to use against Titus."

"Like your reasons for finding them are so much better." She rolls her eyes. "We're all standing here at this godforsaken warehouse for the same reason. And those Imitations we've got stashed share it as well. No one's forced them."

"And that reason is . . . ?" Linc asks.

"Freedom from the creator," she says, looking at me. I say nothing, though my stomach flips at the thought, and she continues more hesitantly. "Daniel's intentions are good. Or at least they started out that way. The grief of losing his mother hit him hard. Knowing she could've been saved."

Saved? And then it clicks into place. Died of myeloma, the tablet said.

"An Imitation," I say, "He wanted an Imitation to save her."

Melanie ducks her head, talking to the ground. "She needed a bone marrow transplant but there were no matches. Titus refused to grow a product for her. He wanted to use her illness against Senator Ryan as a bargaining chip for political reform. Negotiations took so long there wasn't time to grow an Imitation for her. When she died, Daniel vowed to change things. Make owning a product more public, more accessible. No longer under the control of a single dictator." Her words are no more than a whisper, as if she feels the pain of the story herself. "Somewhere along the way . . ."

She doesn't finish, but I refuse to acknowledge the compassion in her expression as she speaks of him. Ultimately, Daniel sees Imitations as nothing more than a means to an end—*products*—and I will not feel sorry for him.

"And him wanting me?" I ask. "Was it just to antagonize Titus?"

Melanie looks back up, eyes glassy with what might be tears. "Yes and no. You were different." There is something in her voice . . . guilt.

Beside me, Linc makes a noise that is a growl and a curse all at once.

"How?" I ask.

Her expression is full of something I don't understand when she says, "You make him crazy."

Linc snorts his agreement. She glares at him for a moment

and then turns to me. Her expression softens. It is the nicest look she's ever given me. "Not like that. I mean he's crazy about you—about her. When I look at you, all I see is *her*. He loves her. And I hate her."

I blink at that—and decide to be honest. "We have that in common," I say.

We share a look.

I can feel Linc watching me, questioning. He doesn't understand what's not being said. That for once, Melanie and I have found common ground. "What is the point of telling me all this?" I say finally.

"Bottom line? I'm offering you the one thing you want."

"You have no idea what I want."

She crosses her arms. "In a word? Freedom. But that's complicated." She nods toward my arm. "You can't just walk out. Not with that thing still in you. I'm offering step one."

"Which is?"

"The location of your friend Anna—and all of the others like her."

I am leery. "What do you want in return?"

"Free Daniel," she says, her voice fierce. "I've heard enough about Titus Rogen to imagine what it's like for Daniel in there. Interrogation, torture, starvation. Titus won't let Daniel die. He'll just make him want to." She goes quiet.

There's nothing I can say to convince her she's wrong.

"Anyway," she says, blinking her way back to the moment. "That's the deal. Help me free him and I'll give you the address. And, in time, a way out."

Linc's answer is immediate and final. "No." Melanie doesn't

look surprised. Nor does she argue. "You can't expect us to risk something like th—" Linc begins.

"We'll do it," I interrupt.

He gapes at me. "Ven, it's imposs—"

"It's worth the trade. Save everyone, or save no one," I say.

Melanie presses her lips together and nods appreciatively. Linc shakes his head but doesn't argue anymore.

"Thank you," Melanie says.

I ignore that and ask the question I can't shake. "Why help him at all? You said it yourself, he's crazy about *her*."

She cocks her head sideways, cutting from Linc to me in a knowing look. "Love is reckless."

By the time we part ways, I have an address.

"Do you think she was telling the truth?" I ask Linc as we climb back inside the SUV.

"About which part?" he asks, adjusting his mirror and easing us into reverse.

"The address," I say, starting small.

Linc makes the turn that will take us back to the highway. Back to Rogen Tower. "I think we'll have to wait and find out," he says.

As we drive, my thoughts are disjointed, incomplete. I am human. Somewhere in the city, Melanie has a warehouse full of Imitations. All of them have found a way to disable or remove their kill switch. I am human. She was helping Anna all along. And others like us. If she is telling the truth, there is scientific data suggesting I am just as much human as someone womb-born. I am human.

I am human?

"When can we check out the address?" I ask.

Linc glances up at the sky, at the sun tracking toward the far horizon. "Not today," he says. "It's getting late and Titus is expecting you for dinner."

"Tomorrow?"

He glances at my arm, at the spot I know my GPS is embedded in. "I'll do my best," he says. His hand leaves the steering wheel and curls around mine, a silent promise.

I blow out a breath, my hope plummeting as I remember what we're up against. "All of this hinges on Daniel not giving it away before we can get there," I say. "Do you think he'll talk?"

"I don't know," Linc says honestly. "Titus is ruthless."

"If they're where she said, we'll have to move them. If he finds them, he'll kill them all." Linc nods. I know he's already thought of this. "You don't have to help me," I add.

He looks over as we coast to a stop underneath a red light and frowns. "I'm not letting you do this alone."

"Linc . . . maybe you should." He opens his mouth to argue, but I hold up a hand and press on. It needs to be said. "Whatever is at that address is my problem. But it doesn't have to be yours. The risk you're taking—"

He interrupts, his voice rising. "Is mine to take. I'm not letting you do this alone."

I bite my bottom lip and my voice breaks as I say, "If Titus finds out you're involved, he'll kill you."

"He could try," Linc replies fiercely.

My eyes water. "He might kill you anyway."

"Why would he do that?"

My heart beats erratically against my chest but I say the thing I'm scared to say. "Because, sooner or later, he's going to realize I'm in love with you."

I wait for his expression to change, for dismay or anxiety or something like it to sweep his features, but instead a slow smile creeps across his mouth and he leans over the armrest so that our faces are almost touching. His hand cups my cheek. "Say it again," he whispers.

"Titus might kill—"

He shakes his head. "Not that part. The other thing."

For some reason, I feel incredibly shy. I force myself to look at him and slowly, I repeat the words. "I love you."

He brushes my hair aside and presses his lips to my cheek. "Again."

"I love you," I say with more confidence.

He lifts his lips from my cheek, presses them to my neck. "Again."

I'm smiling now. "I love you."

He continues to press kisses to my jawline, slowly making his way to my mouth. I say it three more times before our lips finally meet. I can tell by the shape of his mouth as it finds mine that he is smiling, too.

I am breathless and tingling when he pulls just far enough away to whisper, "I love you, too."

The light changes. A car behind us honks impatiently and Linc leans away. He is grinning as he hits the gas and we shoot forward.

Joy, bigger than anything I've ever experienced, surges into my chest. It is a feeling so solid, it seems tangible. If this is what it's like to be human . . . and then I realize . . . this is what it's like to be me.

Ven. An Imitation in love.

CHAPTER TWENTY-SEVEN

SHARP DRAFTS OF wind cut through my hair and sneak into my helmet, caressing my cheeks. The sun sends a swath of light between the skyscrapers, casting shadows along either side of the street. The motorcycle thrums as we accelerate out of traffic, and despite the bite in the air, I'm warm inside my jacket. Any other day, the experience of riding with Linc would be thrilling. Today, it is impossible to enjoy.

The anxious thumping inside my chest threatens to drown out the hum of the motorcycle's engine. Not for what I've left behind. Between Election Day and his prisoner, Titus was distracted enough to let me go without much explanation this morning. He thinks I'm going to vote, an amusing lie when the system is rigged anyway. The anxiety that coils is anticipation for what we're headed toward. I can't shake the feeling that today will change everything.

Red brake lights dot the road ahead, but Linc barely slows as he darts around bumpers and weaves between commuters. In no time, we navigate through the congestion and break free onto the roads that lead to the outskirts. These streets are far less traveled.

Inside my pocket, the scrambler device beeps silently as it redirects my transmitted signal. At this moment, I'm sitting on the back of Linc's motorcycle on the edges of town, but according to the scrambler I'm also having brunch in Dupont Circle before I cast my vote.

We slow for a right turn. The sign mounted on the closest building is chipped and weathered, barely hanging on to its steel frame. I can just make out letters that spell "Weaver Ship" before it's lost behind me. These buildings are long and squat, three stories at most. None of them display numbers so we do a lap and circle back.

Linc slows and raises his visor. "You see it?"

"No."

He angles toward the shoulder and pulls to a stop. I slide to my feet and remove my helmet, shaking my hair free. Beside me, Linc removes his own helmet and stares up and down the street, frowning.

"What?" I ask.

"It's . . . empty."

He's right. Not a single vehicle—not even foot traffic—penetrates from the main road. The quiet is eerie. Almost too still.

"Do you think—?" My words are cut off by a scraping noise. I whip around but there is nothing there. I stare at a corner of the building I can't see around.

The scraping comes again, like feet dragging. A face appears at the very edge of the wall, two eyes peering at us from around the corner. I go still. Slowly, the face emerges far enough that I can make it out. "Anna."

Linc and I share a look. We are here.

"Anna," I call again, louder.

She steps clear of the corner and waits there. The minute I move toward her, Linc's hand is on my wrist pulling me back. "Wait."

"Linc, it's her. Melanie was telling the truth."

"We need to be careful," Linc says. "Let me do another check, make sure we're not being watched."

I want to argue, to run right over to Anna and hug her, but I know Linc is right. Even with all of our precautions, we must be vigilant. I hold up a finger to Anna, signaling for her to wait.

Linc keeps close to the buildings as he slips to the end of the block and back, scanning the street view first and then the rooftops as he returns to my side. I find his hand, wrap it around mine, and hold fast. Linc is winded as we cross the empty street, but his breaths are silent.

Anna watches us from the shadows, her eyes darting in every direction as we approach her. I can feel the tension in Linc as he squeezes my hand. I force mine to remain relaxed—a sign of my own certainty, though I'm not certain at all. Not with Anna biting her lip and looking for trouble behind my left shoulder.

"It's good to see you again," I tell her with forced cheeriness.

At my words, the lines in her forehead smooth over and her shoulders relax. "Same," she says on an exhale. "I wasn't sure Melanie would come through. Will Titus know you were here?"

Linc and I both shake our heads. "I've redirected her tracker. It will look like she was downtown all morning," Linc says.

"Okay. Come on," she says, satisfied. "I'll show you the way in."

We follow her deeper into the alley. Shadows grow and then cross, throwing everything into a murky twilight even though it's not yet noon. We pass a set of Dumpsters that leave a stench in their wake. My nose wrinkles.

Empty crates and debris litter the walkway. I step over several until I'm forced to go around a larger set. The scraping sound from earlier comes again, and I spot the reason. Anna waits in an open doorway. The metal frame has a thick coating of rust. It flakes off in tiny slivers, reddish dust motes in the rotten air.

Warm, stuffy air hits me the moment I cross the threshold. The scraping comes again as the door slides closed. Anna leans on it, shoving with her entire body. She grunts and heaves until the latch clicks shut. Then she slides a giant deadbolt into place.

We're sealed in.

I try not to think of it that way. I think we could open it if need be. But there's no way we could exit in a hurry. I try not to imagine possible reasons for a quick exit.

"This way," Anna says.

Linc blocks her path before she can move. "No way. We're not going any farther until you give us some answers."

"Melanie should've—" Anna begins, but Linc cuts her off.

"I don't trust Melanie," Linc snaps.

"Linc," I mumble.

He sighs. "But Ven seems to trust you."

Anna's expression tightens but she nods. "I understand your concern. Melanie can be . . . self-involved." Linc snorts. Anna ignores it and presses on, "Everything will be explained, I promise. But first, I want you to meet someone."

Linc's voice is lighter when he asks, "Who?"

"His name's Morton. He's been out of the City longer than any of us. Whatever questions you've got, he's the one with the answers." She shrugs. "I'm just a guest."

"How many of you are here?" Linc asks.

"A lot." Linc opens his mouth, probably to argue for specifics, but Anna shakes her head. "I'm not giving you that kind of information without assurances. Talk to Morton first. Then I'll tell you what you want to know about the others." Her voice is firm, her gaze unwavering as it holds Linc's. No one breathes. The silence echoes around us. I squeeze Linc's hand.

Finally, Linc exhales and his shoulders relax. "All right. Take us to Morton."

A darkened hallway winds to the right. Anna leads the way, our steps muffled by a thick coating of dirt on the floor. The air becomes heavier the farther we walk. Even the silence seems muffled. We pass several open doorways leading into small, boxy rooms. They must've been offices at one time. Now they're empty, save for the secondhand sunlight filtering in through high windows.

Anna stops at a gray door with rusted-out hinges. It's open halfway and she pushes it wide with her knuckles as she knocks. "Morton," she says, though I can't see over her shoulders to whom she's addressing. "They're here."

Furniture creaks and feet shuffle as someone rises. More shuffling and then Anna moves aside and I see him.

I blink and force myself not to step back. The man before me is dark-skinned and ridiculously tall. He is easily the largest man I've ever seen. Not large like Marla—large like someone has taken boulders and placed them underneath his skin. There are defined mounds where his shoulders and biceps should be and sinewy veins running the length of his forearms. Through the fabric of his shirt, his chest is broad and hard like the rest of him. Despite his formidable size, he is smiling.

"Ven," he says in a deep baritone. "It is an honor to meet you." His words are accented with something soft I don't recognize. It makes him sound only slightly less scary than he looks.

He holds out a hand three times the size of my own. I take it gingerly, expecting to be crushed under his grip, but he is surprising delicate with me. Rough calluses line his palm and scrape against my skin. He drops my hand, the smile still in place though somewhat smaller, like a secret, when he turns to Linc. "And you must be the bodyguard I've heard so much about."

"I am with Ven," Linc says in a clipped voice. The words are meant to be a simple agreement to Morton's statement but a ripple of pleasure goes through me at what else he's implied.

Morton nods. "Please, come in and sit." He gestures to a faded loveseat underneath a high window. "I'm afraid our accommodations aren't the nicest in town."

He doesn't wait for Linc or me to comply before he turns to Anna. "How's the arm, *mon amie?*"

"It's fine," Anna insists.

"Let me see." His tone is a gentle rebuke. Anna, head hanging, lifts her arm to Morton. He shimmies her sleeve up and peels away the bandage that covers the place where her GPS should be. His face scrunches as he inspects the raised wound. "When was the last time you changed the dressing?"

"I don't remember," Anna says.

Morton sighs. "Anna, you know my equipment, this facility,

isn't sterile. You need to be cleaning it properly. It's on the verge of infection."

Anna sighs. I suspect she's heard all this before. Morton presses the bandage back into place. "Go see Rudy. He'll help you clean it and apply a fresh dressing until Melanie can visit and look at it."

"But Ven—"

"Will be all right," he finishes. "Come find us when you're done and you can show them around."

Anna promises she will and then slips out. I scoot closer to Linc so our legs press against each other and take his hand again. Morton's done nothing threatening, but it's difficult to not take notice of how much space he fills.

Morton lowers himself into the creaky desk chair and links his fingers, resting his hands over his abdomen. "I am not sure what Melanie told you about us but I am very glad you've come."

"She said she's been helping to hide you from Titus and the rest of the Authentics," I say slowly.

"True enough. She's helped us a great deal." It's obvious from the tone of his voice there is more he isn't saying.

"But?" Linc prompts.

"Melanie's what I call . . . an aggressive thinker. She would like to see more action, I think, than the rest of us are looking for just yet."

"What are you looking for?" I ask. It is a bottom-line question. One that, depending on the answer, will decide my role here.

"The same thing you're looking for," he says. "Freedom."

"But you don't want a fight?" Linc asks. Morton shifts to look at Linc and I can breathe again.

"All too often, fighting leads to dying. I want to live. To enjoy my freedom."

Linc's shoe scuffs against the dirty floor. "So you hide here? In a vacant warehouse? Doesn't seem like living to me."

"Linc," I say.

"No, he's right," Morton says. "It isn't much. But it's better than Twig City. And it's better than playing a role for the Authentics."

I nod. Even though this place is dank and dirty and makes me itch, he's right. I'd rather live here than with Titus any day. I ask the second-most important question. "How did you get away?"

Morton rubs a hand over his cheek and chin. I hear the scratch of stubble against his rough palms. "From my earliest days in Twig City, I remember feeling . . . conflicted. I would act all of the right ways in front of the Overseers. Give my best effort during physical activity. Eat right. Say all the right things to my Examiner. 'I was created to serve.' I had the whole spiel perfected. But something inside me was drifting another way. I doubted. I didn't like my purpose. I didn't like being told what to feel—or that I couldn't feel at all. I wanted to be more. Do more. I wanted a choice."

He pauses long enough to catch my eye. His expression is deadly serious. "Do you have any idea what I mean, Ven?"

"I do," I say, my voice barely above a whisper.

He continues. "They call it a deviation. I was the first. Or the first to deviate and live anyway. I was four years made when I received my note from Marla. It was the scariest piece of paper I'd ever held. I think even my bones shook on the walk to her office that day."

Linc squeezes my hand. Maybe he suspects how hard this is.

"My Authentic is a professional athlete. A prizefighter, they call him. Apparently he's also prone to a bad temper and over-indulging in his drink. One night, he argued with the wrong person and was subsequently stabbed. My mission was to take his place in the hospital so he could recover safely, without the threat of someone coming back to finish the job. I must've done a hell of a job playing my part in the City because when I got here, I was shown to my hospital room and left alone except for medical staff. Four days later, in the middle of the night, I got up and walked out."

"What about your GPS?" I ask. "And the kill switch?"

He shows me the underside of his forearm. A small white line mars his chocolate skin. "They are both built into one device. I used the hospital's tools to remove it."

My jaw opens. I am a little disgusted but mostly impressed. "You cut it out yourself?"

"They injected me with pain medication for a stab wound I didn't have. I didn't feel a thing. At least not right away. I managed to keep infection out and eventually it healed."

"Then what?" I ask, enthralled by his courage.

"I found my way down here to the outskirts. The people here are poor but they have heart. Not like the people in Raven's world. Still, I was repeatedly recognized, mistaken for my recovering Authentic. I sought out vacant apartment buildings and warehouses, and I stayed there until something—or someone—made me move on."

"How long ago did you leave?" I ask.

"Five years."

"You've been hiding down here for five years? Alone?" I am awed and saddened by such long-term loneliness. In my case, five years is literally a lifetime.

"I haven't been alone for some time. Although we are always looking for new friends." He smiles, encouraging me.

"You want to be friends with me," I say, my words somewhere between a statement and a question. "Why?"

"You can help us obtain our freedom."

I grimace, despite the hours I've spent contemplating the idea. In reality, it's a lofty notion. "I don't see how there's anything I can do. Titus watches me—"

Morton holds up a hand, cutting me off. "The creator is evil. He wants to use us and if he cannot, he wants to crush us. Don't you want to be free of him?"

"Yes. I want that more than anything." I stare at the scar on Morton's arm.

"Good, because I don't think we can do it without you."

His words are not what I expected, not what I came here hoping for. "What is it you want me to do?"

"Melanie is the last Authentic among us. She's spent the last year exhausting her resources in order to help us live in safety. Now that Titus has Daniel, it's only a matter of time until he finds out about this place. I know we must move, but I am out of locations large enough to accommodate our group."

"I don't see how I can help. I'm not Authentic."

"True. But we need someone on the outside. Someone who can move freely. Someone with access to the creator himself."

In truth, I'm not surprised. But I can't help the disappointment that washes over me. I know what he's asking of me. He wants me to go back. To play my role. My chest sinks into my stomach. I'd hoped for instant freedom, braced myself for the idea of a blade to my arm. But this . . . this is asking so much more.

Linc twists his body so he's facing me. His free hand cups my cheek and he leans in. "You don't have to do this. We can find someone else. We can take your GPS out. They did it with Anna, they can—"

"No, Linc," I say to stop him. "I think . . . I think I have to do this."

"You don't." He shakes his head violently. His gaze is pleading, determined, impassioned by the idea of escape.

I give myself three more seconds of disappointment—for both of us—before I blink the wetness away and stick my chin out. I look at Morton first, then Linc. "I want to matter, Linc," I whisper.

Linc's jaw tightens and I know it's determination for what we're both agreeing to. His shoulders sag. "I know."

I face Morton again. "I'll do it until I can't anymore. That's all I can promise."

His tone is a mixture of pleasure and regret. "That's all I can ask."

"How many are there?" Linc asks.

"Honestly, I don't know anymore," Morton tells him. "Our numbers keep growing. More and more Imitations are being put into place. In the last few weeks, Daniel brought home a new Imitation every couple of days."

"I still can't believe that asshole is one of the good guys," Linc mutters, shaking his head.

"I know he tried to bring you here against your will, without explaining anything," Morton says quietly. "And while I don't condone his actions, unfortunately good and evil aren't as black and white as we'd like. The methods always look muddy to bystanders. I would do anything to protect my people. To some, that might paint me as evil. To me, it means standing up for the ones I love."

I decide Morton must not know the full extent of Daniel's actions, how he killed Gus and used an Imitation in his place, or he wouldn't be so quick to defend him. But maybe Morton isn't entirely good, either. It's something to consider but it doesn't change my decision. Because he is right about one thing. These are my people. And I will do what I must to protect them.

"Everyone here has had their GPS removed?" I ask.

"Yes. Before they are allowed to enter. But yours . . ."

"Will have to stay," I finish, hating the way the words taste on my tongue.

"For now," Linc adds. I send him a grateful half smile.

"No one will suspect you of helping Ven in this?" Morton presses. It's a point in his favor that he's concerned enough about Linc—an Authentic—to ask.

"Not today. Titus is busy with Daniel. And work. There's something big happening at RogenCorp." He shoots a glance at me. "And he trusts me right now, which is how we got away alone."

"Excellent."

Someone raps on the door and pushes it open. Anna walks

in, a fresh bandage on her arm. "Oh, good, you're still here," she says when she sees Linc and me on the loveseat. "So, are you going to help?"

"I'll do my best," I tell her.

She smiles and I am reminded of our morning interactions back in Twig City. Something in my chest yanks sideways. "Morton," I begin slowly. I select my words carefully; the question matters just as much as the answer. "Do you think . . . I mean, when you say freedom, are we speaking only of the Imitations on the outside, or the ones still in the City as well?"

He regards me very seriously and gives his cheek stubble another long rub before answering. "I am certain that we cannot free one without the other."

His words wind through me, a vine leaving seeds of hope planted along the way. I think of Ida and Lonnie, and for the first time since leaving, the ache in my chest doesn't feel terminal. Morton and I share a smile.

"Can I show them around now?" Anna asks.

"Please do," Morton says. "I'll catch up in a moment."

I walk close beside Linc as we follow Anna down a wide hallway with concrete walls. The air here is stale. I try to imagine living cooped inside these damp walls every single day.

"I'm really glad you stayed," Anna says as we walk. "I was so afraid you'd leave after Morton told you everything, after he asked you to keep playing Raven."

"It wasn't a difficult decision," I say. "You all are my family. If I can help most from the outside, that's what I'll do."

We pass through an archway and the space opens around us. The walls on either side extend far; I can't make out the graffitied words on either end from where I stand in the center. Weak light filters in through grimy windows two stories above my head. It is enough for me to see that we are no longer alone—and far outnumbered.

My feet lurch to a stop even as Anna continues into the room. Beside me, I hear Linc's intake of breath. It matches my own. Whatever number of Imitations I'd expected to see, this is far greater.

The warehouse is full.

Many of them are in the process of rolling up blankets that have been laid out on the floor. One by one, they rise and stare, their faces a sea of curiosity and wariness. The soft expression on their faces, the void in their eyes—absent of exposure to the world—tells me every single one is an Imitation. In this moment, I cannot remember why I ever doubted my purpose. *Freedom is the next best thing to being human.*

I become aware of how hard I'm squeezing Linc's hand.

"It's all right. Don't be afraid," Linc murmurs.

"I'm not afraid," I tell him honestly. "I'm home."

ACKNOWLEDGMENTS

I THINK IMITATION is like a cat, because it's already had multiple lives.

In its first life, it was only a concept born from exploring my local library, so, first, I must say thank you to Princess Anne Library. I love the wandering and the smell of ideas in the form of shelved books.

In its second life, a massive thanks to my very special group of beta readers who gave me the feedback needed to plug holes and bring these characters to life: Angeline, Adriane, Desiree, and Christina, you guys rock! To my original editor, Jennifer Sommersby, you made me frustrated in the best kind of way because you challenged me to polish what I thought was already shiny. I'm a better writer for it. Thank you—and don't listen when I whine. Thanks to Angeline Kace for finding such a stunning cover. It's Ven, exactly.

And in its third life, unending smiles and gratitude go to Lanie and Eliza, my editors at Alloy. You guys made me do happy dances regularly with your Team Linc comments and swooning editorial notes. You also made me stretch myself over and over again as a writer. Thanks for the exercise, ladies! I have learned so much from working with you!

I am forever impressed and awed by the efforts of my street team, Heather's Hotshots. You ladies go above and beyond in your support of me, and I thank you. I'm pretty sure some of you were pimps in another life. Just sayin'.

In every life, including my real one, so much love for my minions. You two are rock stars for understanding when you need to eat noodles from a wrapper for dinner and let Mommy work. Playing video games on the couch all day is such a hard life—and I love you for it as high as I can hop.

And lastly, to the real-life Crawford, words cannot express my thanks for introducing me to motorcycles. It is a piece of me I didn't know I was missing. So are you.

SINCE 2011, HEATHER Hildenbrand has published more than eight YA and NA novels, including the bestselling Dirty Blood series. She splits her time between coastal Virginia and the island of Guam and loves having a mobile career and outrageous lifestyle of living in two places. Follow @HeatherHildenbr on Twitter or visit her at www.heatherhildenbrand.blogspot.com.

Looking for more great reads?
Turn the page for an excerpt of the sci-fi adventure

REBEL WING

By Tracy Banghart

EIGHTEEN-YEAR-OLD ARIS'S LIFE falls apart when her boyfriend is drafted to fight on the front lines of Atalanta's war. She has no idea when—or *if*—she'll ever see him again. So when she's recruited to a secret program that helps women fight in the all-male Military, she leaps at the chance. The only catch: She'll have to technologically disguise herself as a man. . . . Just how far will she go to be with the boy she loves?

1

HIGH ABOVE THE olive groves and blinding white roofs of the village, Aris danced. She twisted and dove, guiding her wingjet straight out over granite cliffs and the glitter of the ocean. As she did, she imagined its wings were her arms, reaching far out into the blue. Her fingers would knife through a wisp of cloud, and the moisture would linger against her skin, like a kiss.

Her father wouldn't approve of such thoughts. To him, flying was a practical pursuit, for dusting crops or traveling from place to place. Their village was built high on carbonate stilts, so wingjets were the easiest form of transportation unless you were working the land or hiking down the steep paths leading to the narrow beach below the cliffs. Most everyone here could fly. But no one flew like Aris did.

At least Calix understood what flying meant to her.

She pressed the pedals under her feet and twisted the hand controls, diving in a last tight pirouette before nosing the tiny two-seat wingjet toward home.

A flicker of light caught at the edge of her vision. She glanced out to sea and steered the wingjet in the direction of the movement.

Suddenly, the flash became a speeding wingjet. It hurtled toward her, its silver sides reflecting the sun. Aris hovered just off shore, the beach a golden crescent beneath her, waiting for the wingjet to change course or slow to land. Instead, it grew larger, advancing quickly. Surely the flyer saw her? Her hands tightened on the controls. She moved farther from the cliff. The other wingjet shifted too, keeping her directly in its path.

Aris nearly waited too long. She jerked the controls down, the force of the other wingjet's passage rattling the bones of her machine as she locked into a downward spiral. Heart beating wildly, she waited until the last second before pulling up and skimming the water. Beneath her, waves rolled from deep blue to white, ruffled by her jet wind.

The other flyer followed, matching her move for move. Her stomach twisted as the wingjet drew up alongside, giving her a clear view of its needle nose and the Atalanta flag decal stretched across its sloping tail. No solar panels curved above its wings like on her wingjet. Instead the whole thing shimmered a silvery gold, the hallmark of new-tech solar material. Aris had only ever seen Military wingjets on news vids, never up close.

What was it doing *here*, so far from the front lines of the war?

Without warning, the jet shot upward, piercing the cloudless sky like a shining arrow. She slowed to watch its progress, waiting for it to disappear. But with a flash of reflected sunlight, it dove again, straight for her.

What is he trying to prove? Her apprehension shifted to annoyance. She darted out from under the jet and flipped through the air to face him. It had to be a *him*. All members of the Military sector were male.

For a moment they hovered in a strange standoff. Then the other wingjet rocketed forward, forcing her into a series of evasive spins and loops. At first Aris dipped and whirled away in anger and frustration. But gradually, his movements lost their aggression and she relaxed into the dance, pushing farther and twisting faster until it was suddenly *her* chasing *him* across the sky. *She*, who flew the most intricate patterns, she who nipped at his jet wind, whooping as she tumbled toward the flashing waves below.

Eventually, the other flyer slowed and headed back to the cliffs, tipping his wings in a "follow me" gesture. She watched him land, her heart still hammering, then followed suit.

As she touched down, the tall, yellow-flowered grass beneath her swept in wild circles. She wrenched the hood-release lever twice before the glass slid back. It always stuck a little—the hazards of a second-hand machine. Not that she was complaining. Her parents had given her the wingjet three months ago for her eighteenth birthday. It was *hers*, and the only thing she owned that she really, truly cared about.

Aris slid both hands through her hair, trying to smooth it down. She'd left it loose and curling, the way Calix liked, but her recent maneuvers had given the heavy auburn waves a reckless disregard for gravity.

The other flyer stood among the flowers, waiting for her. Dressed in full uniform—blunt-toed boots, trim pants, sleek forest-green jacket—the man represented every fear she had for Calix. On the back of his neck was the black rectangular brand that marked him as Military. He could have just as easily appeared in a news vid as in one of Aris's nightmares. Her breath froze in her throat, and her hands went cold.

"That was incredible." The stranger was slight, with a fine-boned face and thin lips turned up in a smile.

"Thanks?" she replied, taken aback by his enthusiasm.

"Really, I mean it. I've never seen anyone go from a right-hook flutter pattern straight into a flat-nosed full spindrop."

With a grin, she said, "I call it the swing zinger."

He laughed. "I'd heard you were good, Aris Haan, but blighting hell, that was *fantastic*."

A whisper of unease unfurled in her belly. "How do you know who I am?"

Instead of answering, he held a hand up as an invitation. "You coming down from there?"

Her weak leg tensed reflexively. Flying was one thing; getting in and out of a wingjet gracefully was quite another. She eyed him warily. "Why don't you answer my question first?"

The man's friendly smile twisted into a guarded expression. "It's not important."

"And how did you know I was here? Is *that* important?" she pushed.

The man shrugged. "I watched you leave your father's grove and followed you so we could speak privately. And so I could see what you can do."

Her mind raced. He'd followed her? How had she not noticed? And more importantly: "Why would you do that?"

"Because I want to offer you a job."

She let out a disbelieving laugh. Not only were women not allowed in the Military sector, they weren't authorized to take *any* job, in any sector, deemed "dangerous." What could he possibly have in mind?

"Tomorrow, at your selection, you'll be invited to join the Environment sector," the man said. "And then what? Work as a duster for your father's groves? There were only two people in your entire year that scored even *close* to you in the aviation trial. That talent would be wasted there."

His words sent ice down her spine. "How do you know I'll be selected for Environment? No one finds out their sectors until the ceremony."

"I know more about you than you can imagine," he interjected. "I know why you won't get down from that wingjet, for one. And I know you'll never fulfill your potential here. It'll eat away at you, settling for this life." He put a hand on the side of her wingjet. "Listen to me—"

"Who are you? Is this some kind of . . . I don't know . . . some sort of trick?"

He raised his chin. "No. And I don't offer this lightly."

"You're Military. You can't be . . . I mean, you can't offer—"

"You have a lot of questions, of course. But I'm not the one to answer them." The man drew a small piece of silco from his pocket and handed it to her. The letters on it were stamped in blood-red ink. "Go to Dianthe. She'll explain everything. You'll find her at this address in Panthea. Tell her Theo sent you."

Aris took the silco, gingerly, as if it might bite her. "You want me to go to Panthea?"

He leaned closer, a new urgency in this voice. "Don't tell anyone where or why you're going. Tell them you got a job in the city, whatever will keep them from asking questions. We'll set it up, however you need. No one can know what you're really doing. It's imperative that you tell no one. Do you understand?"

She studied Theo's face. Understand? He had to be joking. "I don't understand *anything*. What kind of job is it? And why do I have to lie to my family?"

"This is your chance to fly," he said, his eyes serious. "Not that mindless drudgery you do for your father. I mean *real* flying. All across Atalanta. You have no idea how useful you could be to the war effort. How many lives you could save."

She couldn't keep a burst of bitter laughter from escaping. "That kind of flying isn't useful. It's self-indulgent." Her father had told her so often enough.

He made an impatient noise. "I've watched you. I know what your life is like here. Why aren't you jumping at this chance?"

Anger spilled through her. "You don't know anything about me. How dare you spy on me and think you know me? I'm happy here."

"Really? You're happy being a duster and never leaving Lux?" Theo stared up at her, his face set in rigid lines.

"I am." With Calix, she would be.

"You're either stupid or selfish then." He turned away, as if disgusted with her. "This isn't just about you."

Selfish? Stupid? "If you know so much, surely you're aware I'm about to be Promised." She and Calix had already decided. Two years of Promise, then they could choose to marry. And be bound, irrevocably, for the rest of their lives. It's what she'd wanted for as long as she could remember. "He's going to ask me tomorrow, after selection. I can't leave, and there's nothing selfish or stupid about it."

The man turned back to her and scoffed. "A Promise? Don't count on it."

"Excuse me?" Shock painted her words.

"I assume you're referring to Calix Pavlos?"

Her chest tightened. "Tomorrow he'll join the Health sector. He's going to work in his mother's clinic. We—"

Theo slammed a hand against the side of her wingjet, cutting her off. "Have you not watched the news vids? This war will claim us all, one way or another." His thin lips twisted with an emotion she couldn't identify. "Calix *will* be selected for Military, make no mistake."

"You're wrong." A buzzing filled her ears. "We're winning the war. *That's* what the news vids say. Calix isn't going anywhere." This man was her nightmare after all, come to take everything from her. "His family has been part of the Health sector for generations. There's no chance—"

"There is, Aris, and you know it." Theo stepped back, tipping his head up to look her in the eye. "Please. Consider my offer. You could save lives. Maybe even Calix's."

Then, without another word, he climbed into his shining wingjet and sped away.

For more, follow @tracythewriter on Twitter
or visit her at www.tracybanghart.com

Looking for another great read?

Turn the page for a sneak peek at

EVERY UGLY WORD

By Aimee L. Salter

SEVENTEEN-YEAR-OLD ASHLEY WATSON can't walk through the halls of her high school without bullies taunting or shoving her. She can't go a day without fighting with her mother. And no matter what she does, she can't seem to make her best friend, Matt, fall in love with her. But she does have something no one else does: a literal glimpse into the future. When Ashley looks into the mirror, she can see her older self. But her older self is keeping a dark secret. Something terrible is about to happen to Ashley. Something that will change her life forever. Something even her older self is powerless to stop.

CHAPTER ONE

AS THE PSYCHIATRIST enters the room, he offers me a patronizing smile. I return it in kind.

He indicates for me to take a seat, then sinks into a worn leather chair, looking just like a doctor should: graying hair, well-trimmed beard, and wire-rimmed glasses I suspect he doesn't actually need.

We face each other over a glossy, mahogany coffee table. While he flips through my file, I scan the room. Shelves of creased paperbacks line the walls. The single window is framed by subtle drapes. There are doilies under the table lamps and two doors on opposing walls. This office resembles a living room—if I ignore the bars over the shatterproof windows. Kind of kills the good-time vibe.

Doc clears his throat. I take a deep breath and turn back to him.

"How are you, Ashley?" His voice is too loud for the muted tones of the room—all earthy browns and soft corners. The quietly ticking clock in the corner tells me it's 9:34 a.m. That gives

1

me about five hours to prove I'm normal and get out of this place once and for all. Five hours until *her* life goes to hell, if I don't make it home in time. I focus on him, try to smile. It's already been a rough morning, but I can't tell him that, not yet.

"I'm okay." I shrug, then freeze. My stitches are only memory now, but searing pain lights up along the hard, pink lines spider-webbing across most of my upper body. I breathe and wait for the jagged bolts to fade. My surgeon says I'm healing. But he forgot to mention that to the layers of mangled nerve endings beneath my fractured skin.

"Pain?" Doc's eyes snap to mine. The benign disinterest was an act. He is measuring me.

"It's fine. I just moved wrong," I say breezily.

My physical scars aren't the reason I'm here. He can't fix those. But he can help me by letting me out. As head of this facility, no one leaves without his approval.

I mentally shake myself. He *will* let me out today. He must. If I can get home in time, I can fix . . . *everything.*

Doc's lips press together under his perfectly trimmed mustache. After a second he smiles again.

"I see you brought your bag."

The duffel bag my mother packed before dumping me here six months ago sits on the floor like a well-trained dog, as ready to go as I am.

"Yes."

"So you're confident about today?"

"I'm confident that I'm not crazy."

Doc's smile twists up on one side. "You know we don't use that word in here, Ashley."

2

There are a lot of words they don't use in here. *See you later,* for example.

I take another breath. Cold. Calm. Sane. "Sorry."

He returns my stare, face blank. "I'm glad you feel confident. However, I do have concerns."

"Concerns?"

He smiles in a way I'm sure is meant to be reassuring. But when he sits that way, with the overbright anticipation in his gaze, it kind of makes him look like a pedophile.

"Ashley . . . you've changed therapists three times during your stay. Do you know what I think when I hear that?"

I think the question is rhetorical, but he waits, expectant.

"Um . . . no?"

He hasn't looked away. "I think as soon as anyone gets close to the truth, you flee."

I can't break my gaze without confirming his suspicions. So I swallow and wait.

His calm is maddening.

When he speaks next, it's in the cool tone of a professional shrink. "I've read your file, spoken to your nurses, and been briefed by your therapists. Now I want to talk to you. About this."

He makes his way to a closet in the corner, then pulls out a massive full-length mirror. It stands taller than I am, with a wrought-iron frame that is hinged in the middle, allowing it to pivot. He rolls it in front of the shelves in the corner of the room, far enough behind me that I can't see into it without turning my head.

A kindness? Or a challenge?

Doc returns to his chair and I force myself to follow him, to keep my eyes away from the glinting surface.

"I have a hunch if we examine whatever it is you see in the mirror, we'll find the truth about the rest, Ashley," he says. "I'd like you to stand before it and tell me what you see."

Panic lights up my veins. "What? Now?"

Doc raises a brow. "Unless you have a better idea?"

I don't. I'd expected this session to be like all the others— a glib exploration of my past, patronizing questions about my psyche, along with self-congratulatory compliments when I make a "breakthrough." I was prepared to do whatever it took to get out of here by 2:30, but I can't look in that mirror—not now.

What if she's there? She won't understand why I'm ignoring her. She's been through enough today already. We both have. And breaking her heart is breaking mine.

"The mirror won't make any sense without the rest of the story," I say, trying to buy time. If I can get him talking, show him how normal I am otherwise, maybe he'll decide I don't need to look.

His face remains impassive, but his head tilts to the side just a hair. He's onto me. "I know the story you've fed your previous therapists. If there's more, I'm willing to put the mirror aside for a time—"

I slump with relief.

But he raises a single finger. "—if you tell me everything. There's only one route to getting my signature on your release forms, Ashley. And that's it."

His patience is a marble rolling along a slim edge, precariously balanced between hearing me out and sending me back to that cell they call a bedroom.

4

Swallowing again, I try to make myself pitiful. I drop my head into my hands. "Okay," I breathe into my palms.

"Okay, what?"

"I'll tell you the truth." As much of it as I can, anyway. I'll let him think he's gotten through where others failed. Hell, I'll even consider what he has to say if it means he won't make me look in that mirror.

"Excellent."

"So . . . where do you want me to begin?"

He crosses his leg over his knee, pulling up his pant leg slightly. "Nothing too dramatic. Start with the night you planned to give Matt the letter."

I feel the grin slide off my face. Nothing too dramatic. *Right.* I can't help glancing sideways at the mirror. Doc follows my gaze, and when he sees where I'm looking, he frowns. For a moment the magnitude of what I'm trying to achieve is overwhelming. I cannot breathe. But I force my muscles to loosen. I swallow my fear—and begin to speak.

For more, follow @AimeeLSalter on Twitter
or visit her at www.aimeelsalter.com